Wheelbarrow Ridge

Tom Williams

Wheelbarrow Ridge

& other stories

Acknowledgements

'Raven' was shortlisted for the Commonwealth Short Story Prize, 2013.
'Harmonic' was shortlisted in the Hal Porter Short Story Competition, 2013.
'Returning' was longlisted for the ABR Elizabeth Jolley prize, 2014.

'Cord Blood' was published in *Southerly*, Vol. 70; 'Bridal Veil'
in *Island* 117; 'Chancer' in *Famous Reporter* 44; 'Harmonic'
in *Lane Cove Literary Award 2014: An Anthology*.

Wheelbarrow Ridge & other stories
ISBN 978 1 76041 083 4
Copyright © text Tom Williams 2016
Cover photo: Carole Williams

First published 2016 by
GINNINDERRA PRESS
PO Box 3461 Port Adelaide 5015
www.ginninderrapress.com.au

Contents

Glint

They gaze at the bay as they talk, their faces lit by a thousand glints tossed back by the lapping waves. White sand at their feet, a ragged skirt of golf course grass as a ready place to sit. People pass on the strand below where the surge and hiss of the water's edge shifts out to a greener depth. And they look to where the sea grass beds begin, a deeper blue, but never at each other.

The heave in her chest slows as Jen finds the meter of her words and slowly, Pam falls into silence. She turns to watch the dance of Jen's expressive hands, edges close to her daughter's side, and feels a pang as Jen pulls back. Pam knows she must be strong.

Their first meeting in two years. Pam had disapproved of her daughter's divorce and judged her for having had another man waiting. Jen had railed: on the far side of her mother's hypocrisy an older sorrow lingers. A sorrow that had once been big enough to share but, having been apportioned, turned one against the other.

The fine white sands of the tombola shelve gently. Three younger women are testing out a paddleboard. One stands and the other two wobble the craft, pitching her off amid shrieks and laughter. A German-speaking couple walk past, bare feet in the water as the baby in their backpack waves its hat at the sun.

Jen looks out to Solitary Island as she talks, the cream of sea waves on its rocks, a lone kayaker rounding the headland. She turns and looks at Pam, 'It'd be okay if you'd ever followed your own advice, but you didn't, did you? Not with Dad.'

Pam sighs. She should have known that this was coming. But what to say? How do you reach down through the depth of so many years? How do you describe the intimacy of the unbearable from such a distance? And with Jen, so much like her father. He'd made his own failure, and taken it with him. Jen was all that Pam had saved from the wreckage, though the daughter cannot see it, even after all this time.

Images of unwanted drama and the self-harm of the father come rising up from closed-off places. Pam tries instead to remember the little girl who had been so central to her concerns. A child never meant to understand. She shuts the moment down; there are no words, and it only hurts to ponder.

Did the daughter ever value Pam's love, or just take it as her due? To bridge the gap, Pam reaches out a hand and Jen's eyes are red with anger. She looks at the hand for a moment, takes it.

Jen's voice softens, but her words remain hard. 'Yet you judge me for leaving that moron I never should have married.'

Pam almost says that she had advised Jen not to marry him in the first place, but swallows the words. Having drawn a breath, she says instead, 'I was thinking of the children, dear, and Darren was not the same as your father.'

A southerly breeze stirs dissonance through the masts and cables of a distant marina, carrying away the pause and heat of an early-autumn day.

Jen is momentarily stilled by her mother's words, but it passes in this moment. 'No, not like Dad. Darren didn't need help, he needed getting rid of…you're the one who can't make that distinction.'

Pam winces, seeing back to the smear of blood on bathroom tiles and the binding up of wounds. Looking straight ahead, she whispers, 'You were a small child, Jen. You're in no position to judge.'

'Yeah, that's your role,' replies Jen.

Unobserved, Pam's teeth bite her lip. The waves begin to slap the beach, and each one leaves a pattern that the next one sweeps away. It was Jen who had sanctified her father's departure, but Pam who let her, not wishing to disabuse a little girl's loss.

But where the wounds of the father had gaped, they were also self-inflicted. The salving of a precious child's mind had become Pam's surviving priority. She looks at Jen now, a woman nearly forty, still ensnared by that unstable past and, lost for words, turns away.

Two of the paddleboarders stand knee-deep in the water, calling out encouragement to the third, who comes wobbling back against the wind. The kayak has rounded the ferry pier and comes on, drawing slowly nearer.

She sees the paddles flash as they catch the sun and says, 'Jen, if I've hurt you, I'm sorry. Whatever advice I've given you about your personal life, whenever, it was only ever my intention to encourage you, not to… repress you.'

'That's such a generic apology, Mother, and brief. But I seem to remember that you repartnered yourself pretty quickly.'

Pam huffs to herself. Repartnered! Really! Is it that simple? The daughter is about to speak again but Pam interrupts, 'You didn't completely know him…' and is cut off in her turn.

'I got in touch with Dad last year! He visits me here sometimes.' Jen nods towards her home beyond the cove.

Pam follows her gaze, exasperated: she has travelled three hundred kilometres to visit her daughter, wondering, hoping, why Jen has called. But she hadn't planned on travelling back in time. She regards the architect-designed homes across the water, discreetly sited amid graceful trees, imagining a homeless man trudging up to any such designer door, and finds herself inclined to scoff. She looks back and holds Jen's eye, 'Oh,' she says, 'and does your new, um, partner get along with your father?'

Jen draws back her lips, exposing her own teeth without humour, expelling a breath that falls short of words. They stare into a deepening silence as tall clouds gather beyond the bay, and the young women share the weight of the paddleboard as they walk in step to the road.

Pam wonders about Jen's father for a moment, whether he copes with his problems now, or still self-medicates until he wakes, surprised in a psychiatric ward. But the subject is too far off the point. Jen's own needs had always been mercurial enough: the havoc she'd caused in the second, step-family, the later succession of dubious gurus who had slowly led her nowhere. It was good that Jen had never taken to the bottle like her father.

But there had been just so many, all-too-important people in her life that it was a wonder to Pam that Jen's marriage had lasted as long as it did. No, perhaps it was those people she drank dry: flattered at first as Jen acquired their tendencies and mannerisms, upset as her devotion wandered. Of those Pam had happened to know, all had been dumbfounded when their time arrived to be shown the door. One or two had rung in search of explanations, though Pam had none.

No, for her to call me here now, thinks Pam, after two years of silence, there must be some new upheaval in her life. She nurses the silence and moves her hand on top of Jen's, waiting.

They face a sun that has passed its zenith and its tilted rays rebound and dazzle off the restless heave. Shadows slant the steep, opposing shore as the kayaker sweeps his craft in an arc across the glint, turning for the beach and surging in to land. The darkness of the young man's face is played with light by an intimacy of waves.

Jen's hand jerks and stiffens. Pam turns to see what's wrong but Jen has turned her face away from the shore.

She removes her hand from Pam's and puts it to an eyebrow. 'We should go and get a coffee,' she announces, standing abruptly with the hand still raised and her back to the beach, looking anxiously instead towards the café by the pier. And without another word she strides away along the strand, and as she strides the sand beneath her feet is yelping.

Pam drops her hand onto her lap, confused. Rising, she takes a step towards her daughter, then glances back to where they'd sat to check that nothing's left. As she turns again to follow suit, she sees the paddler by his boat. The kayak bumps against his leg but he watches Jen, one hand raised in a frozen greeting. He calls her name to no effect as his face falls flat from surprised delight. Pam's face is pointed at him so he probes her with a look that she understands too well: why, he appears to wonder, why did she do that?

Pam decides she does not want to know. She looks along the strand to Jen, waiting at a distance. No, thinks Pam, and nor am I meant to. I'm wanted here for what, blame, unquestioning support, both? Moving past the stranger, she straggles along the sand. And it dawns on her, if her daughter always had unstable needs, she has never wondered why, she has only ever blamed herself. She stops again, looks to the road where her car is parked, turns to face the daughter.

Of Glass

His shortcut turns out to be a mistake and Lim looks around, failing to recognise a single building. The streets all curve and sweep; he can find no order in them. And the houses sprawl too big with rubbish in the yards: engine parts and mouldy chairs, children's toys half-chewed by dogs. Move away, he thinks, move on.

He spins around, but which way? This foreign sun, so low, is set wrongly in the sky. No. He stops himself. This is the new order, it is I who must adjust. He feels the cold and turns his collar up, but in his mind sees Bandalong again, and the fire, flaring on the water, roaring. Already lost to sight, had they called out to him as the flames reached them? How could I have done so little, he thinks. Move on.

A man with tears marked in ink comes walking on the footpath and Lim turns to face him. 'Piss off, slope,' says the man in passing.

Then the trumpet of a railway horn sounds distant to the right, so Lim resumes his walk towards it.

Luxford Road keeps curving left and Lim turns right at Shipton. There is a low-slung school and houses, proud with neater gardens. A four-wheel drive is pulled up on the footpath and he steps around it, but bumps a chair that holds a leaning stack of homeware: papers fall and scatter, and picture prints in plastic frames that crack and clatter, and beyond the shatter of their glass, one bronze vase that gongs the path and rolls. It stops at the opening of a gate.

Beyond, a lady looks up from the darkness of a doorway. 'Ah, jeesers,' she shouts. 'Can't ya look where ya goin?'

'Sorry, so sorry,' says Lim, scrabbling to collect the frames, standing them by the gate.

The lady approaches, past some roses, so Lim grasps the vase and stands to pass it to her. Something clatters from it and chinks upon the concrete. He looks down and feels a momentary shock, for looking back with unblinking gaze is an eyeball on the footpath.

But the lady breaks his spell, erupting with a wheezy laugh and shouting at the house, 'Hey, Sharnie, looks like we found yer granny's glass eye!'

Lim bends towards the gazing eye and lifts it on his palm.

Trundling from the house comes a rubbish bin, and behind it, Sharnie, blinking. 'Huh?' she says.

'Found yer granny's bloody glass eye,' repeats the lady, looking grey and straining with an out-thrust chest as her laughter grows wet edges.

Slowly, respectfully, Lim extends his palm with the eye balanced upon it, and Sharnie steps around the bin and lifts a rose to peer, myopic. Silence extends the moment, bar one train that rumbles.

And Sharnie lifts her gaze to Lim. 'Ah, yair,' she says, uncertain, then shuts Lim's hand with hers, closing it on the eye. 'Why don't ya keep it, mister? It'll bring yer luck!'

He reopens his hand to assess the weight of the object, to feel its place upon him. Not inanimate or precarious, it does looks well positioned, unlikely to roll or fall. It has a presence that he could not expect. In looking at it, he has a desire to follow its gaze, away to one side.

Sharnie loses interest, and the other lady, purple-faced, has forgotten all her laughter. Hands on hips, she totters as she fights to find each breath, the noisy rails of which have dampened down into an intermittent squeak.

Sharnie lights a cigarette and offers her a toke.

Lim thinks only of the eye. It is obvious that these two will not take it back, and even if he were to place it respectfully on the gatepost, they would simply throw it in the bin. Ah, he sees, the eye is gazing at a rose which hangs heavily over the path. He notices its scent for the first time, and moves the platform of his hand towards to its fleshy petals. But a harsh curl of cigarette smoke coils around him and he looks up to meet the impatient gaze of Sharnie.

'Yair?' she says, one hand on the slumping back of the older lady. Then, with exasperation, 'Bloody yair, you still here?'

Lim backs out the gate with his hand, and its burden, proffered towards the women. By the time he stands beside the road, the older lady has wilted to a floppy seat upon the ground where, snagged, the rose has bent to watch her.

Sharnie takes an awkward grip upon her tuck-shop arms and is leaning heavily back while muttering past her durry, 'Bloody get yer arse off the deck.'

But the lady's arms are flaccid, and her head lolls. Lim, however, sees that the gaze of the eye has turned away from this scene, and points now in the direction of the railway. He closes his hand respectfully upon it and strides off, feeling the glass grow warm.

Many people board the train at Parramatta and Lim finds himself increasingly uneasy, crowded up against the window. People sway in the aisle, absorbing jolts off the tracks, all moving in unison. Or, seated close together, search their phones for threads to link their lives to other places.

Only Lim, he is sure, is so entirely alone within this throng. And so he thinks of Bandalong again, and the train jars. He tries to jump his mind clear, but lands straight back upon the rail track of his memories, which speed him on towards despair.

Beside him once more, Tseu stands above the water, extending her arm beyond the deep, thatch shade and he watches, enthralled by the sinuous sway of her ngaweh dance. Until she glides her sun-warm hand back from the light, sharing its glow with his own cool hand. The tenderness of her kiss, a touch of foreheads. In lifting up her face to his, she laughs and says, 'Were you not on your way to work?' For months, his parents had spoken of the changes taking place in the kampong, but Lim had paid them little heed, for the old will always ruminate so. Although he had observed the strangers, and had meant to pass the mosque before the end of morning prayers.

The tight clench of his hand grows painful and there is a stone there which draws him back to the swaying carriage. He finds himself dizzy from the labour of his lungs and, still alone within the crowded space, uncurls the fist from around its burden. Impassive, the foreign eye looks back, green, cooling from the heat of Lim's passion.

A voice enters his thoughts from the right. 'Are you well, sir?' it calmly enquires.

He closes his hand quickly and turns to face the speaker. An ageing Sikh is seated next to Lim, his coal-black eyes warm with concern. They flicker with restraint as Lim's fist descends to his lap. No mention is made of the eye. Lim bobs his head in answer to the question, lowering his own gaze, embarrassed.

'Very good, sir. I am not meaning to be rude, sir,' continues the Sikh uncertainly, but the words only tumble into the space separating the two men, increasing the gap. 'I am hoping, sir, that you have not missed your station,' he continues inventively, looking for a courteous exit.

'No,' answers Lim after a pause. 'I go to Bondi. I am working, for cleaning.'

'Ah, very good, sir. I too am working, in the city. Today, I shall drive a taxi,' exclaims the Sikh proudly. 'But,' he continues with one finger lifted, warming to his audience and leaning across the gap, 'it is not a thing I will do for very long. Indeed not. A colonel of artillery I have been for many years, in India, and soon I shall find here positions more suited to my rank.' He sits up straight again, adjusting the lapels of his jacket.

The man's solicitude is a distraction that eases Lim's emotions. He turns his face to the colonel again and nods, saying 'Yes' in order to continue the exchange.

A scent of napthalene drifts easily between them.

'And you, sir, are you a supervisor, in this cleaning?' asks the colonel.

Unable to discern the meaning of this question, Lim looks slightly to one side and whispers 'Yes' once more, with another, slighter nod, and then extemporises haltingly, 'They say I am working hard. Soon, I am given, uh, passport back. I stay then, not sent back to Sulawesi!' He stops and examines the colonel to see if he has been understood.

The colonel lifts his head ramrod straight, staring sternly back. And his voice is shot with gravel as it growls, 'Passport? They have your passport?'

'With visa,' Lim interjects. 'I here to work. They bring me. Place to live and they give. When give passport back, they pay. No work, sent back. I am good.'

'Fuckers,' exclaims the Sikh, tightening his lips and looking at Lim fiercely. And the black eyes of the Sikh begin to smoulder, with their rheumy whites-gone-yellow now intershot with red. He lifts a hand as if about to pass advice or further judgement, but pauses. He sighs, and Lim can feel the man's gaze cool as it passes through him, as if the colonel has suddenly lost sight of the substance of Lim, or sees instead a person only slightly visible, translucent, of glass. Shaking his head, the colonel lowers his hand, and sighing once again, looks fixedly to the fore.

No more words are shared amid the scent of napthalene.

As the carriage shudders and roars, Lim can feel another gaze, within his hand. The crowd sways as it races within a brutal silence. He puts the eye in his pocket.

All the flats had been empty, except, in a way, for the last. Some appeared unoccupied, with just a rime of dust on expensive, unloved furniture. Others appeared to house many, poorer people who slept on floor-strewn mattresses, but rushed away to work. Lim is indifferent and concentrates on a mantra to calm his troubled thoughts: 'Cleaning, I am cleaning well,' he whispers as he wipes and lifts, vacuums and mops. And for many hours his mind is calm, until, in one final room, he works beneath a topeng mask. Hand-carved for the tourist trade, never meant to be worn, the snarling mask hangs from the wall as a memento of its absent owner's Bali holiday.

Lim pauses, looking up, and suddenly sees Tseu again, laughing as she holds a similar mask beside her face at the theatre in Bandalong. He wrests his mind clear and is met again by an eyeless gaze, the empty slits looking outwards and inwards with equal disdain. Lim stares inside them, finding only shadowed space and a wall. But a flicker grows there as his mind returns to flames, with his home ablaze on stilts above the water. And all he has, or could ever love, is trapped within. And caught in desperation he turns for help to a crowd of onlookers. Outlined against the night, their faces are lit by the fire. Faces that he has known all of his life, gone to school with, bought fish from at the markets. Not the strangers from the mosque who have gone off in search of other Chinese homes to burn, but faces that he thought he knew, staring back like masks, impassive at his loss.

Lim drops what he is doing and walks from the flat, closing the door upon the following gaze of the topeng mask. He stands for a time on the landing, holding the bannister to steady himself, wondering why his lungs still breathe and his heart still beats when he would only have them stop.

But Lim abides within the emptiness of the landing and realises in time that he has no choice but to go on. So he searches himself in case he has left anything important behind in the flat, which he does not wish to re-enter. And he finds the eye, heavy in his pocket, and grips it in a sudden flare of rage. He lifts his whitened fist, opening it first to reproach the sightless object, then to fling it down to shatter upon the marble of the ground-floor entrance.

But before he can cast the eye down, the ground floor door swings open and a woman enters, dressed in black. Lim stays his hand. She ascends through the gloom of the stairwell, whistling a formless tune to which the ageing timbers of the stairs respond with creaks and groans. On the top landing, the woman in black encounters the unexpected form of Lim, and the hand he holds before his face is clenched. Her eyes widen.

Lim turns his rigid face towards her, and sees there two eyes that exactly match, in colour and pattern, the green one that he grasps. His mouth falls open, even as her lips unpurse from their whistle.

And she smiles at him as his words falter, and says, 'Oh, you must be the cleaner. I've been hoping to catch you sometime. Just don't have time for, you know, cleaning. Courts have gone bloody mad, flat's a pigsty half the time!' She pauses for a moment and Lim's mouth works but doesn't speak, so she smiles again, and the lines beside her eyes are shot with absent laughter. She speaks more slowly, 'Suzie,' she says with a nod and one hand to her chest, then, with more hand gestures, 'If you want extra work, come in and we can talk about the arrangements.' She turns and opens the opposite door, steps inside and looks back at Lim, still smiling as she waits.

He pauses, lowers his fist and crosses her threshold through a derangement of thought and emotion.

She closes the door with a click. 'Hey, Lee,' she calls down the hallway, 'I've caught up with that cleaner, but I'm not sure he speaks much English. You wanna come and see if you can speak to him for me.'

'I already tell you, Suzie, I do all cleaning,' a voice calls back from the lounge room.

'Yeah, yeah,' says Suzie, 'and pay rent and study and work. But it's my flat anyway, and I'm paying, so you gunna come and speak to the guy or not?'

'You gunna start charge me market rent then, Suzie?' replies the voice.

'Try not to be a nong,' responds Suzie. 'Just come and do the talking, will you. It's what you're good at!'

Lim observes that the flat is very neat.

A young woman of east Asian appearance rounds the end of the hall, lowering a book to a table. 'So you speak English or not?' she demands of Lim.

'No so good, little,' answers Lim, shuffling, affronted by her directness.

'Zhongwen?'

He shrugs.

'Hokkien, Hakka?' she persists, and he nods as much as his lowered head allows.

'Ha?' demands Lee.

'Hakka,' murmurs Lim, the word distorted by a twitch of his lip.

'Okay,' says Lee, turning to Suzie with a shake of her head, 'I no speak to him better than you, girl. He from Indonesia or somewhere. They got own language there. He go now?'

'Jesus, not so fast,' says Suzie, exasperated. 'He doesn't bloody need to talk, does he? Just clean!'

Lim wonders if he is visible to these people either. His lowered face hardens like a mask, and he lifts it suddenly and growls, 'You want speak me, you talk me!'

'Oh. So sorry. Wasn't thinking,' says Suzie, still oblivious to all but her own thoughts. Concentrating on her words and testing a small, awkward bow, she continues, 'Did not, mean to, be, rude. Do you, have, hourly rate?'

Lim guesses at her meaning as his frustration swells, catalysing other, older emotions that swirl and meld, simmering to the surface of his deepening rage. Suzie's bright stare nettles him further and he feels it too, within his hand, blind to understanding, indifferent to his loss. He realises that he will no longer bear such callous scrutiny. His fists begin to clench and unclench.

Thus, the eye of glass is released and bounces once upon the carpet. Robbed of words by this unexpected sight, it is the turn of Suzie's mouth to stay open, her eyes lowered to match a cock-eyed stare. Lim's face, raised, has assumed the contortions of the topeng mask next door, blind too, with anger.

Lee gawks at the fallen eye and steps forward, crouching into its glassy line of sight, her nose wrinkled with surprise and distaste. She follows the eye's line of vision to a plaster cornice, looks back at the hand that dropped it and, finding it clenched, follows its arm back up to the contorted face of Lim. His eyes are blinking with tears that catch the light as he turns his face to hers.

She straightens, mystified, taking the hand unthinkingly within her own. 'You okay?' she says, softening at the sight of such despair.

Lim looks down upon her upturned face, her hands, the first to hold his own since Bandalong, and his fierceness crumbles. As the contortions of his face collapse, Suzie blinks and forgets the eye that lies upon her carpet. Stepping forward to join with Lee, she puts her hand upon Lim's back. His sobs unleash as they lead him down the hallway, and a footfall weighs upon the carpet as the glass eye rolls to watch them.

The Cleaners

Think we could try somewhere else next time, she says, smoothing back his damp hair, sighing when he fails to respond. There, that's better, she adds with quiet persistence. You're not really bald at all you know. You shouldn't worry so much, luv.

His Adam's apple flips up and back, so he must have heard that, thinks Charlene. But he's too far gone with his phone to respond. She hears the tram clanging below and thinks how late it's got, thinks too of her flat in Rozelle, so cheerless, even with the new leather lounge suite, and reaches out again.

Dal pulls his head back across the pillow in a spill of sparse, grey hair, then rolls to face her, bringing the phone up between his face and hers. You fucken bastards, he growls at the phone, scrolling in a series of jabs, cursing the screen as it jumps from subject to subject.

Tuh, she says through a small gust of breath, swinging her legs over the edge of the bed and sitting up. She feels his trickle and wishes she'd reached for a tissue, but arches her back instead and flicks her hair, straight towards him, then stands and looks sideways at the mirror, cupping her new breasts. They, look, great, she thinks. She can see him in the mirror too, or at least the back of his phone. Couldn't keep his hands off 'em, she purrs to herself, disappearing into the en suite.

Dal Ekhardt is filthy. That little squib Strilbert's after the cleaners again, he shouts. And hearing only silence, adds, Shaz, what were those photos Edso said he had? He looks up, finds her gone and hears the shower running, closes emails and sits up slowly with one hand held protectively to his back, crouching, dizzy, until the sight of his feet resolve from a head spin. You'll be the death of me Shaz, he adds through a deep wheeze that erupts into mirth. Then, hacking, he stands. He takes a cautious step that's still unsteady, kicks one bottle that clangs against another and puts one hand on the bed as he works his way around a narrow space.

At the door of the en suite he talks into its steam. Luv, think I've sunk a few too many, better not drive. Di's gunna flip again if I don't get home. Guy's covered the meeting for me, but she could still ring up. You know what she's like. Think I'd better get the train. He sees his pants on the floor and flops back onto the bed, pulling them on commando, then struggles into his half-buttoned shirt. Shoes by the door, still got the socks on, tucks himself in, and he's gone.

Charlene emerges from the steam a few minutes later, ample, pink and unsurprised by his absence. It takes her eighteen minutes to squeeze herself back into her work clothes and realign her hair. She checks the room, dropping his forgotten underpants into the bin, rolling his silk tie and placing it in her handbag, then, scanning side to side, closes the door carefully behind her.

The staff in the office are frantic, rushing to assemble the final presentation of an award application.

With ill-sorted provisions half-negotiated, they have been caught short by the Industrial Commission's decision to expedite their case. Phones jar and email threads confound, and each worker takes turns to yell, some for advice or to jog a memory, others to shout 'Shut up'. But such furore is barely discernible from the mezzanine suite.

Charlene has rolled the visitor's chair to the back of Dal's desk and is helping him pore over a sheet of small photographic prints, hand-delivered in a plain envelope five minutes earlier. Dal is rumbling and hrooming with laughter, his index finger pressed firmly on one image.

No, says Charlene, and get your finger off it, they're bloody film, you know, not digital…

He lifts his heavy finger clear and she continues, Yes, I know the girl's pretty, and I see what she's doing, but that's not the point: this shot here is the one that shows his face, the only one.

The phone on Dal's desk rings and he picks it up, unspeaking, his eyes still riveted on the first photograph.

Charlene leans across and hears the febrile voice of Guy from downstairs, complaining that, by his calculations, the hospital cleaners' pay deal will fall below the inflation rate. He gabbles off a list of statistics as his voice amplifies, finally finishing with a nearly hysterical question. What the bloody hell, he wants to know, is he supposed to do when the cleaners are already threatening to walk?

She lifts the unheeded receiver off Dal's palm and replies, Look, Dal's already told you, as long as they hang onto their call-off meal allowances, they're still ahead!

She doesn't need the phone to hear Guy's response. I told you, his shout echoes up, we traded off all their allowances last year, Christ, they don't even get lunch any more!

Moron, she mutters as she hangs up, looking back at the still distracted Dal. Now where were we? Oh yes, turning to the photos. You can see what Strilbert's doing too, in this one, and if you can't see so much of her, that's a good thing: keeping her out of it'll keep Edso happy. He might want to keep her profile low. Good girls don't grow on trees, you know!

Yeah, s'pose, says Dal slowly, wresting his eyes clear as he swivels his chair around to face the window, resting his heels on the sill and looking down to the traffic below. You made that appointment with Larson yet?

She responds primly, It is only ten in the morning, you know, but yes, though he wasn't keen on it. I just explained how it affects the premier and that changed his tune. Looking at her watch, We're expected at parliament house in one hour and twelve minutes.

Yeah, the premier, growls Dal, and Strilbert, his little bloody helper. Thought the house'd be sitting, though? He tilts his head and turns it, fixing Charlene with a cool, grey stare.

Larson said he'd come out, knows it's urgent, she replies, putting the sheet of images back in their envelope before looking up to meet his gaze. If you're not happy, you might have rung him yerself… And then, thrusting up her chin, You're such good mates.

Dal blinks heavy eyelids as he gazes at her, catching his bottom lip between his teeth for a moment, scraping it. Well, ya better book the bloody taxi then, he drawls at last.

Already have, she replies, turning her head away with a flick of hair.

Mate, I don't want any bloody arguments, Dal shouts at the taxi driver, leaning forward to brandish a credit card in the man's face. You take bloody American Express or not?

Oh, most certainly sir, very good, sir, replies the driver, waggling his head.

Idiots, mutters Dal, turning to Charlene as he settles back in his seat, holding up the card as he adds, And how the bloody hell did we end up with these useless things anyway?

She exhales audibly, pauses as she looks out the window at a gaggle of kids being shepherded by a pair of frazzled teachers, looks back and replies, Actually, you negotiated the card package, Dal, and there's not a lot of general secretaries with such a generous credit card deal, funded by their office cleaning contractor. So can we get on with the business?

Not a lot of cleaners get paid like those bastards either, he says, and this is the best they can come up with?

Although Dal's fuming appears to be directed at the back of the driver's turban, Charlene resists an urge to elbow him, and swallowing an admonition about the other, hospital cleaners whose union fees supercharge the card's unlimited credit, says Yes instead. But what do we offer Larson?

We? Dal turns and lowers his ill-humour onto Charlene: Oh yes, we have our own card too, don't we? That doesn't mean that we fucking well get ahead of ourselves, do we? You just sit there pretty, Shaz, and shut up.

Another group of schoolchildren are crossing William Street towards the museum. The driver runs a red light, blaring his horn and they scatter.

Dal smirks into his phone for a minute, punches out a reply and resumes his study of the driver's turban. Did you remember to bring the bloody photos, he asks it.

How's the Dalek, asks Larson as he strides down the rear corridor to meet them.

Hands in pockets, Dal Ekhardt tosses his chin, aiming the gesture at some shaving cuts on the pitted face of the health minister. Fine, pineapple face, he replies. Didn't get that electric razor I sent ya fer Christmas?

Smart arse, answers Larson as he steps around Charlene without acknowledging her presence, opening the door to his office and, leaving it wide, striding across to his desk.

A tall woman comes out of an anteroom that fronts the public corridor and he says, Beat it, Gwen. Go get yerself some lunch.

Silently, Gwen disappears back into the room from which she has come.

Larson sits and nods to the single chair in front of his desk. Dal is seated swiftly, ready for business, with Charlene looking around, confused.

That's fer you, says Larson, looking at Charlene and pointing towards the still open doorway through which they have just entered. Shut it behind yer.

Her face reddens, she looks to Dal but he's swivelled his chair and faces the minister. She struggles for words but Larson speaks again, to Dal. Incidentally, thanks mate, fer putten' the mockers on those bloody hospital cleaners, health budget's stretched, I tell you.

Absolutely! Budget bloody emergency, mate, understood, replies Dal as Charlene begins to walk silently towards the door. But Dal turns his head and stops her with an outstretched hand. Hey, he says, snapping his fingers. The photos.

Charlene hands the photos over wordlessly, trying to maintain her dignity as she turns and walks swiftly to the door. The first tears well as she shuts it behind herself and she leans against it for a moment, hearing a faint burst of laughter from the two men in the room. But another door opens further up the corridor and again she sees Gwen, stepping forth in a smart suit. Gwen pauses, looking at Charlene as if she might offer some aid or advice. But Charlene turns her face away and, pushing upright off the door, follows with her body, walking tall on her awkward heels towards the stark daylight of a distant entrance.

Her phone rings, she looks at the number and it's Guy, so she moves to kill the call, but changes her mind and flicks the screen.

His voice charges straight out of the device. The cleaners, he's shouting as if being attacked with a mop. I gotta speak to Dal but he won't fucking well answer! I gotta meeting in thirty minutes with all the state delegates and they're filthy, say they're gunna break away, go over to the Sundry Workers. What the fuck am I gunna do? I gotta speak to Dal!

Dal bloody Ekhardt, she finds herself hissing, then in a rush, You speak to me, Guy, now!

Dal returns to the office in a fine old mood. Ah jeez, he says, sitting unsteadily on the edge of Charlene's desk, you shoulda seen the look on his face.

Charlene smiles back coolly from her chair and asks as if she cared, When he saw the photos?

Nah, nah, he replies, waving a hand and shaking his head. Then, pausing the hand and looking up with dewy eyes, Well…actually, that girl… But he breaks free of his reverie and waves his hand again, continuing, Nah, he's swallowed the whole deal, Shaz. Yew wouldn't believe it: Strilbert's sunk! Him, his little Sundry power base, with all their mops and bloody buckets. And come the state conference, with their membership numbers so far down, they'll amount to nuthin'. I tell ya, I'm gunna go after their accreditation.

Charlene settles deeper between the armrests of her chair, propping her elbows and joining her hands in front of her lips as if holding back a prayer. Wish I'd been there to see it, she says mildly to her palms.

Ah, ya woulda loved it, Shaz. Had Larson eating out of my hand: deal is, he takes the piccies to the premier, see. Says, look, we gotta do something bout old Strilbert. Pretends he's got the snaps off a reporter that's hot on Strilbert's trail. Dal guffaws, miming the action of picking up a photo sheet and bugging his eyes in terror.

Charlene titters politely.

So, premier cuts loose his numbers man, I get that bastard off my back, and you'll love this bit, Shaz: the very next day, Larson announces he's outsourcing all hospital cleaning contracts…

But, they're still our members, says Charlene, confused.

Yeah, yeah, but Larson's got this old memo from the premier's office, see, asking him to do a costing on a privatisation of the whole sector: thing was just a kite, poor old bastard probably doesn't even remember sending it. Anyway, I start jumping up and down about it with the press and when the heat comes on, Larson holds up the memo, says fer the record, Bloody premier's made me do it, you know, my hands are tied… bit like old Strilbert with that girl, huh?

Dal throws his head back to laugh at the ceiling before continuing. Ah, brilliant part is how I come in like high dudgeon, white knight, stoking it all up big time with the threats about going out on strike…

But what about the award negotiations, she interjects. Won't they be compromised? Industrial Commission's not gunna like it.

Huh? Dal seems confused for a second. Nah, get real, Shaz! Getting rid of Strilbert's the issue, helping Larson get the premier's job, that's the issue: could be a bloody Senate seat in this for someone!

Someone, repeats Charlene blandly. So what do you want me to do about it?

You just get yer pretty self down to the bottlo with yer Amex, and get us a couple of the best: Dom Perignon should do. Then book us a room fer the night. The best room, down at the quay. You're worth it, luv!

Charlene works patiently with a nail to draw back the plastic cover. She pours a few drops of long-life milk over some brown granules already in her cup and stirs them, but they resist dissolution. She persists, whisking at them guardedly with her plastic spoon until they surrender, adding boiling water from the jug, then the rest of the milk before a final, leisurely stir. She takes a sip and sits back with her steaming cup of Lustrous Tiger Café, then sets the cup aside and re-ties her bath robe, hugging herself as she leans forward to watch ferries pass in and out of the quay. First slant of morning sunlight, warm against the air-con chill.

Oh yes, she remembers, fishing a container of sleeping pills out of her pocket and lowering them gently into her handbag. Doesn't want them rattling. Only faint intimations of city traffic penetrate the room, the muffled beep of a horn, a deeper rumble that she feels from the passing of a train. But it is the presence of Dal Eckhardt that dominates the space, even from a deep sleep, with his wet and ragged snoring.

She sips again then puts her cup down between the two smartphones on the glass table, quietly, avoiding any slop of coffee. She picks up both the devices but has to hold them at arm's length to compare the inboxes, and shift back out of the sunlight. Gotta get some reading glasses, she thinks with a sigh. Nice ones.

It's nine-thirty. Her own phone displays two strings of correspondence that began the day before, connecting her by email to both Guy and Strilbert. Goodness, she thinks as she reads Guy's latest message, talk about task-focused. Give that boy a job to do and things do get done. Another email arrives from Strilbert and he's still sour, but less suspicious than when she first contacted him. Surely, she thinks, a hint of gratitude wouldn't hurt. But his prose remains superior. Yes, the premier is fully informed, and also, the executive committee of the Sundry Workers have indeed reached their decision and are willing to establish a new branch for the cleaners.

Cleaners, okay, done, she thinks, forwarding the message to Guy. But pauses as she re-examines Strilbert's email: Premier, fully informed. Charlene glances nervously over her shoulder.

Slowly, the hulk in the bed keeps heaving, even through its chainsaw-rip of snores, so she moves her gaze back to Dal's phone. Most of his emails are from Larson, plus all the missed calls and texts. The last text is two minutes old and its wording is succinct: Fucking pick up, you cunt! She purses her lips, double checking that the device's vibrate settings are also turned off, and toys with the idea of emailing Larson yet another blokey reassurance, but decides it's getting late.

Dal becomes apnoeic, then breaks out into an eruption of snorts.

Should get going, she thinks as he farts and jerks against the resistance of his tangled sheets.

But another email comes in for Dal from the premier. Although at least this time she doesn't need to dream up a reply: less guarded and probing than the messages that preceded it, it contains neither demand nor outright threat, consisting instead of just one cryptic statement: If the Dalek has been bad, exterminate the Dalek, exterminate!

Charlene forgets the steaming coffee and turns off Dal's phone before dropping it into his jacket pocket, then looks around for her clothes.

Bridal Veil

She locks the car. There's only the letter left to do. She slots it behind the windscreen wiper. 'Dear Dad'.

The air brakes of a distant truck hammer the night, but she is caught only in the glare of memories. They remind her of another presence, the valley. Beyond these trees, darker than the night, there is a barrier of cliffs and then a deeper emptiness.

A breeze crosses the car park, moving from the higher ground of the plateau and carrying its chill towards the precipice, drifting through the handrails of the lookout and falling, unseen and in slow motion, into the valley. Far below, rank upon rank of eucalyptus ripple, waiting.

Her memories are strobes, now revealing the path to those same handrails, now the view from beyond them. She squirms again, all these years later, between the harsh grasp of his hands. Again, his laughter rings in her ears. The more she squirms, the tighter he holds as she looks down into the terrible indifference of the trees and screams, 'Daddy.' The valley gives nothing back. Is her voice too small, or just not worth an echo?

Then there are the falls, the Bridal Veil: a diaphanous shift of water, beauty swaying in tresses through one slow, eternal fall from high bed to low. She remembers too, a day of sunshine and thrilling gusts. Cold spray off the falls, a welter of crystal fragments wheeling in to strike.

In the darkness, she drops the unnecessary keys and turns away from the lookout. Across the car park is the track to Bridal Veil Falls. She finds the first step without holding her hands in front of her. The Parks Service has recently upgraded the path and her feet search out each new footfall without difficulty as her hands glide dew from the rails. Voices of anguish and reproach are left behind and after a while she hears only the voice of the creek.

The planks of the bridge are under her feet and there is a white glimmer below where the brook skims past. She kicks off her shoes, undresses, folds her clothes and arranges the shoes neatly on top of them. Shivers at the cold of the railings as she slips between. Gingerly lowers her feet into rafts of vegetation that crowd the edge of the creek's clean, stone bed.

There is a scratchy tangle of cushion fern, knee-deep, and she remembers its lichenous smell and the way it made her sneeze. A step towards the creek and she trips, her feet ensnared. The hoary stem of a melaleuca strikes her face, rasping an eyelid and seizing her by the hair. There is the tang of blood on her lip and she can smell tea tree. For a moment she sees her mother, pulling chunks of cotton wool off a paper-lined roll, soaking them in tea tree lotion and dabbing at her grazes, eyes averted.

Then the ferns make her sneeze and she is surprised at the ridiculous hold of this shrub upon her hair. Sprawled and prickled amid the ferns, she can't pull free, so she gathers herself awkwardly into a foetal position, as if in homage to a persecutor, grabs the tangle of hair and pulls back hard. The offending branches snap without warning and she tumbles backwards, all arms and legs, down a small embankment and into the creek.

The water is not as cold as she expected. It has a faint sulphur and iron smell and for a moment she worries about getting this strange odour in her hair. Then she snorts and lies back, spreading her arms and legs wide, looking up and seeing the stars. The bridge is just visible against the slight luminescence of the night sky and her father is standing there, holding her little dress, shouting, 'Get the hell out of that water, right now.' She ignores him and launches one more leaf boat, watching it bob and spin on the sparkling torrent: spinning free on its roiling tide, racing down to the falls, lofting out over the mirror-shard spray. Behind her, his shout becomes a bellow and the small squat of her buttocks and the childish curve of her back become rigid. She knows what that means.

Her hair is free now in the water, it caresses her skin like algae. She sifts out the last of the melaleuca before taking a deep breath and making herself rigid, feeling her torso lift off the ochre-slippery bedrock and pivot at the current's behest. Finally, her feet lift and she floats free. The stars rotate with her, but the ride only lasts a metre or two because, for all its vigour, the brook is small and shallow. She stands and continues downstream. Sometimes the bedrock is so smooth and slippery, and the vegetation on the banks so dense, that she has to get along on all fours. She is walking along a rock shelf on the edge of the creek when she reaches the falls.

It has been a lengthy process – becoming insane – occurring little by little since her childhood and accelerating after the divorce. Alcohol to kill the pain, party drugs to cure the depression, unhinged now for months, her moods swoop and dive like gulls on a rubbish tip.

The presence of the valley exerts itself again. The glimmer of the creek dances and chuckles and then pitches straight down into the great, enveloping silence. Her toes on the edge, she can feel a cold exhalation as the valley accepts this gift. She spreads her arms and it is only a matter of toppling. There are lights in the distance where the mountain towns continue clear through the night. In the far distance is the light haze of the city. Only this valley is hers, this deep, blue sea.

Mania has made a visionary of her. In saner moments, she remembers her father's jibes and is sure that he was right, that she is both stolid and a coward. She reproaches herself now for failing to tumble forwards. She just can't do it. The recent months of depression have separated her from the empathy of others, like being lost at sea, and the struggle to stay afloat has exhausted her. This night must end the struggle. She has come here to do it.

She notices the creek's transitions: its movement from presence to absence, from clamour to silence, how its glimmer becomes darkness. She has an idea and steps back into the water where her feet skid wildly on the slippery scum that lines the bedrock, almost skating her over the edge.

A strangled scream escapes her lips, forming into a snarl as she swears at herself. She drops to her hands and knees and makes her way out to the middle of the sudden spillway. There, she lowers one haunch onto the bed of the stream, extends her legs in front of her and sits, facing the valley. Her feet project over the edge so she wriggles forwards until her knees go over and she can dangle her lower legs. This is it. The stream banks up behind her back like a courteous usher and her legs form conduits as water jets off her toes. To hold her position, she has to use her hands. She can feel the slippery layer under her palms and remembers, from long ago, its rusty colour.

Last night she dreamed of the sea, of surrendering and sinking below its surface chaos. The drift down was easy and graceful in the sway of her hair and the splay of her limbs. But, as the light filtered away, she met a layer in the water, a thermocline, where the clarity of the sea changed across an interface, to the same rusted ochre. She poised above the thermocline and calmly regarded its opacity and utter stillness until, at her least movement, its surface rippled away in all directions. But wait, were there shapes beyond the boundary, did they shift towards her, just below the surface? She had woken in a panic, clawing back towards the air.

The creek's flow has eased her forward a couple of centimetres, so she leans backwards a little and pushes on her hands to reposition herself. Water immediately slides between her and the slippery rock, causing her to lurch. Her hands slide too, just a fraction, like the movements in her dream. This sensation is more horrifying than any nightmare. Her body reacts instinctively, hunching onto the stream bed as if she could grip it, her hands discerning of their own accord, just the right pressure to stop herself. She is aware of a warm sensation. She has peed herself. Nausea and abhorrence roll over her and she freezes, at last comprehending the irrevocability of her actions. Her thighs are halfway over the ledge.

At its mercy now, she imagines the valley revealing its true nature, rising up from below and towering over her as a column of gloom. Its voice is the unsaying of things, a silencing, of the brook, of the rasp of her breath. Its passage brushes the hairs of her arms, her breasts. Its breath on her face is sulphur and iron and, oh, so cold.

Ponderously, the column rotates and gathers slowly to its margins the lights of the towns and the haze of the distant city, spinning the light and diffusing it into a funnel that reveals, at last, the hunger of the abyss that circles at her feet. Her world has become a shrinking margin, rotating upon the edge. She sobs, alone. There is no name to call upon at the end. She sits shivering, waiting to topple.

Whether thirty seconds or thirty minutes pass is academic to the state of her exhaustion and convulsive shivering. When the rescue team arrive, her consciousness is starting to slip and she is close to the end of her endurance. They come, scything the night with disembodied torch beams that converge on her as if from another world, punching her shadow out into the night through sudden, glinting shards. Unable to shield her eyes, unsure of reality, she turns her face away and stares into the tunnel of her shadow.

There are two paramedics and three police, called out to investigate after a call from some lovers who found the woman's letter and abandoned car at the lookout. One policeman has a headlamp and wears rescue overalls; the others, in uniform, carry torches. Surly at this hour, expecting to encounter some sobbing attention seeker, they are appalled. The extreme urgency of the situation is manifest and each of them struggles in a sudden depth of responsibility. They have no rope. All they can do is retreat into the habits of teamwork to hammer out some kind, any kind, of plan. They talk briefly and quietly in a huddle.

One of the paramedics takes off his belt and hands it to the policeman in overalls, who puts it on as he moves to the edge of the falls, calling out to the woman reassuringly.

She turns and stares towards him, wide-eyed, mouthing something incomprehensible, perhaps 'Hurry.'

He calls back to her, 'Don't worry,' and feels like a fool.

Meanwhile, the others pace the edge of the creek until they find a mallee tree on the bank. They mutter agreement. Torches perched on shrubs and rocks, one grabs the mallee's thickest stem before linking wrists with a second who steps into the water on skating feet. He chokes back a profanity, trying to appear calm. A third worker clambers onto the end of the chain, and then the fourth, murmuring anxious jokes about his partner's intimate proximity. No one laughs. Finally, the policeman grapples out and the joker grasps his belt, leaving him with two hands free, facing the woman.

They know they are taking a terrible, unprofessional risk. Their line of approach to the woman is diagonally across the creek. If she goes over, and drags the policeman with her, then at least one, maybe two, will follow as they pivot off the tree and their human chain breaks. Yet they can see that she is too near the end for any other plan, except to simply stand and watch her go.

The man in overalls regards her in the light of his lamp. She is trembling, her face is turned to the darkness and her head lolls. Yet she still manages to perch, stubbornly upright, with almost all of her legs projecting beyond the edge. Her hands divide the laminar stream so close to its launch point that the flow doesn't have time to reunite. She is just beyond his reach. He estimates that if he commits himself to leaning forwards, off his mates' support, he will be able to hook one hand under her arm and assist her to ease backwards. He feels a sense of detachment from reality which scares him more than anything else.

He calls out to her and she lifts her head. For a moment he feels frightened of her as she turns her face towards him. Then he sees her profile, her freckles and remorse. There is an abjectness about her which defies his experience.

She is murmuring, over and over, 'I'm sorry.'

He hates this job, all his years as a policeman. He was never much of a father to his own daughter, who is not much younger than this woman. But it's too late to change any of that. Determination displaces his pity. He warns his mates and leans forward, off them, explaining to her what he plans to do, how he will take her arm and how she needs to stay calm and accept his help by easing backwards, slowly, until he can hold her properly.

Despite their previous agreement, one or two of the others can't help themselves and call out to her too, telling her that 'Things will be all right, luv,' and 'It'll be over in a sec, don't you worry.'

She nods again, out of sync with what is said, and the policeman explains that he is about to touch her and take her arm. He confirms with her once more that she knows what to do, to take things easy, wriggle backwards little by little, only when he says.

She replies, 'Yes.'

He touches her biceps before sliding his hand beneath her arm. She feels the touch and lifts one palm off the rock, desperate to grab his hand. Instantly, that side of her body slips over the edge. She rotates as she falls away from him and a split second reveals the expression on her face, branding it permanently on his memory. The five of them stay poised in their hold on each other, unbelieving, as crystal points stab into the void she has left behind.

The water atomises and decelerates, drifting off to one side in pleats and curtains, veiling her as she plummets straight down.

Chancer

We find him on the track down from The Gut. It's hot as. His shirt's off, he's drenched in sweat and his mate's propping him up as he hops along on one leg. I smell the sharp stink of him and feel sorry for his mate. God, he's filthy.

The good thing is that Maeve now owes me a bottle of Oyster Bay: I don't recognise the patient and obviously she doesn't either. We'd heard from radio control that he's an off-duty paramedic and we've been arguing about whether or not we'll know him. It's not that I actually care. One fat fool snapping his ankle on a tourist track is the same as any other fat fool, paramedic or not. The point of arguing with Maeve is to get her Irish accent going. It's stronger when she's stroppy and I love it when her face goes red and, hair falling over one eye, she calls me a 'feckin eedjut'.

So, she's on the blower checking out how far back the police and the vollos are with the wire stretcher, I'm starting to introduce myself when he interrupts, 'You did the first ascent of Chancer, didn't you?'

I'm taken aback. How does this geezer know anything about me and that rock climb? I notice that he isn't fat. In fact, he's lean as a whippet, has veins like hosepipes: one of the few things I do get excited about these days.

So I answer him, 'Nah, mate, I'm not that old. But I did put up the alternative start to Chancer, and I named it Feelin' Lucky Punk.'

It was only then, courtesy of my variation, that Chancer became an international drawcard for hard climbers. Christ, that was back in 1990, when my son Jack was a toddler. Now, I don't even know where Jack lives.

There are shreds of moss sticking off him like sandflies, bits of fern in his hair and his trousers are saturated and torn. Like hell he's been tramping along a tourist track. I look across at his mate, who avoids my gaze, turns to one side and stares out into the trees. Through a gap in the canopy the big white rock-face of Chancer stands, two hundred metres higher, serene and white, above a humid silence.

At this point, the cops arrive with the vollos and the stretcher and my patient turns sullen and quiet.

The IV access is as good as it looks. I slip in a fat sixteen-gauge for practice and he doesn't even blink. Then, waiting for Maeve to stop ferreting through the kit and draw up the morph, I ask him, 'So, what actually happened?'

He replies, 'I slipped over on the track, crossing the creek below The Gut.'

Yeah, right, I think, giving him the first five of morph that Maeve's finally prepped. We put him in the stretcher and I give him another 2.5 after we've tied him down. Then we pick him up and head off. It's going to take an hour to get down to the road but there's no hurry with his injured foot having a strong pedal pulse.

I drop back in the queue till I'm next to his mate and whisper, 'What really happened?'

His mate says, 'He slipped over on the wet rocks at the creek crossing below The Gut,' then moves away, up the queue.

Feelin' Lucky Punk had been my high-tide mark in climbing. For me, it's as good as things ever got. The hardest route in Westland in its day, it's still a climb that you just can't afford to fail on. And I'm proud of that because it's got the type of cred that speaks for itself. We did it in one push, on first sight and from the ground up. None of your pussy abseil inspection or glue-in-bolt protection in those days! Looking at this young guy in the stretcher now, ground-up and spat out, I snort to myself.

But he's a tough nut and complains not once as we bump down the jungle track, though he's happy enough to finish off the last 2.5 of morph and maybe that's what gets him talking. Or whispering. 'Feeling Lucky?' he hisses when the cops can't hear. 'I was trying to back off from ten metres up, there was rotten rock and a hold broke. I decked out.'

Rotten rock? I feel indignant.

The duty crew are waiting for us at the road and we load him into the back of their wagon. Instead of 'Thanks' or 'See ya', he snarls through the closing door, 'We need to talk.'

That night, the Oyster Bay all gone, I add up all the years I've lived alone. I worry about the anger and shame I still feel about Fiona. I wish I could just let go but it drives me mad, not knowing where she went. The kids. If I could just go back… Anyway, I still climb a bit, and I've got my work and, with all these years gone by, I've earned a 'well known for turning up and dealing with the hard shit' reputation in both fields of endeavour. I think how good it'd be to get out of Greymouth, but it's the last place we were all together… Jack might come back, looking for me.

I shake my head and try to think about something else, pace a bit, pour another Scotch. Turn to the net for distraction. The guy we picked up turns out to be not just a fellow ambo, he's a top-flight international climber. God, the grades he's ticked. And he knew who I was! What does he want to say to me?

We were good in those days, punk climbers feelin' lucky. I remember again the crux sequence out onto that sharp arête from the top of the failing crack, Mark shouting at me to please stop, turn back, for Christ's sake. How I'd pushed on through to the end.

Next thing, I'm back at work and there's a private email for me on the staff intranet. It's him. He wants me to ring him on his mobile. I get straight onto it but his attitude's not what I'd expect. In fact, it's all wrong.

He takes the liberty of telling me that he knows he can rely on me to be 'a gentleman' and not tell anyone what really happened. Okay, I can accept that. Keeping yet another 'climber rescued' story out of the press is a good thing. But, if this guy wants my cooperation, why isn't he being straight with me. He's acting as if he's not sure about anything any more. Even the most basic facts have gone missing. Did he fall off the clean, hard start of Feelin' Lucky, or was he dumb enough to tumble down through the leatherwood and supplejack scrub on the original pitch of Chancer? He doesn't now seem able to recall. That's when it hits me: there's no acknowledgement here, he just wants to make sure no one finds out he fell off my old climb.

At bedtime, I chase down a couple of valium with the last of the gin. When I wake, I'm on the bathroom floor, my back aches and my neck's gone stiff. I can't remember how I got here but I remember the dream that woke me: I'd floated away on a tide, the water just took me. But the further out I got, the gentle splash turned to slap and began to buffet. The water got dirty, all in my mouth, its taste too bitter.

Now, I look into the bathroom mirror and see in that face where the salt taste began. It's three a.m. I'll be gone from this town before the dawn.

Cord Blood

Scores of wattlebirds are scouring the heath. Two burst out of the bottlebrush next to her and hurtle away, clacking and cackling. She wonders if it's love or hate as their harsh cries disappear into a greater cacophony. A second shrub shudders as it swallows the two bolters and she looks past it and sees what she's been searching for.

The tree is in a stand of timber beyond the edge of the heath, its trunk a failed diagonal among the vertical lines. Knocked sideways by a storm years ago, it's perfect. A tough little silvertop ash that has worked hard since its accident, reaching down through the orange soil with its surviving roots, cinching itself back into the bedrock. The crooked branch lying beneath arches back off the ground in one spot but remains attached to the main trunk by splintered shafts of wood. The tree still tries to mend these old, fractured ribs with a bulge of sapwood and it irritates her, this incomprehension of a small battle best lost, the waste of resources.

She forces her way through the heath, determined to test the stability of the fallen branch. There's a ten-metre electrical flex slung over her shoulder, a few loops have slipped free and a trailing power plug snags among the bifurcations of a dead banksia, pulling her up with a start. She turns in sudden fury, yanking the flex with both hands in a series of savage jerks, cursing flex and dead shrub alike with her husband's name, moron who can't keep a rope in his shed.

Eventually, the banksia's brittle arm snaps and she hauls it in like something slaughtered. Savagely, she rips off each and every twig until the flex is completely free. Her hands are bleeding, her face contorted. She turns back towards the tree, panting, and pushes through the last of the scrub.

The fallen branch turns out to have some life left in it. It's stable and springy and curves a metre off the ground. Above, the main trunk of the ash has a projecting branch three metres higher and a metre and a half to one side. It's ideal. It takes her a few throws to get some coils of flex over the high branch and even then she has to use a forked stick to drag the troublesome plug back down. She wants to anchor one end to the main trunk, well out of the way, but there isn't enough flex to do it. Again, she curses the husband, then, for want of any other anchor, ties an end of the flex onto the highest point of the fallen branch. It's hard to get a neat knot in such stiff cable but at last it's done. All that's left to do is the noose.

She has to climb onto the arch of the fallen limb. Conveniently, there's a native currant bush crowding one side of the branch so she climbs up through it, grunting and pulling hard on the dangling end of the anchored flex. Once up, she needs both hands to wrangle the noose and it proves to be a balancing act. Harder still, judging the height for the knot is tricky and requires several attempts. She falls from her high stance twice before the noose is right: a simple thumb knot does the trick best, slipping to and fro easily along the body of the flex. Finally, to be sure, she re-ties the bottom anchor to finalise the height of the noose within the working range she has estimated. Her hands don't shake. She's businesslike. If she doesn't know what to do, she does what it takes.

At last, one hand in the foliage of the currant bush, one holding the noose, she's ready. Hesitating, she looks down to where her feet broke the crust of the ground and exposed a floury loam honeycombed by ants. There are pearly eggs being shifted away by workers and she thinks how in time they'll come to descend the flex and march in line across her face. In and out of nostrils, black, gaping mouth. She looks away.

This foliage in her hand is so heavy with plump, green currants. By way of distraction, she struggles to remember the Latin name of the shrub. Yes, that's it, *leptomeria*, a parasite that grows out of the roots of trees. She looks up, probably this one, leans her head through the loop and launches herself.

At the Oddfellows Clinic in Singapore they had called her the Perfumed Steamroller. She knows she has the guts. It's her hands that surprise her, acting without instruction, gripping the cord above her neck like Tarzan gone awry, yet cushioning her cervical spine from the swing and jerk. But, my god, the pain, the pain is intolerable!

She struggles for a moment to see through it with detachment, even as her legs jig and thrash. Clearly, she sees it is the intention of her lower limbs to hook an ankle back over the branch she has just launched herself from. So, when they succeed, she's not surprised to see those same hands suddenly reappear, seizing the thrumming line of ascending flex and pulling hard.

How disappointing that the surprise effect of this effort is to lift her foot back up and away from the bough. And, without the extra support of her hands, the torque on her throat is fiendish. Rotating now as she swings and thrashes, she hears a pathetic little siren above the roar of her pulse. Is it help arriving? No, she realises the noise is the only element of a scream able to force its way past the noose. Her chest is bursting with the effort.

Having twirled completely around, she gets a heel back over the branch. Thinking quickly now, she grabs the ascending flex again, but pulls in the opposite direction to last time, gaining enough stability to snatch one hand into the foliage of the native currant on the far side of the branch. She pulls now with all her might, cinching a knee forward over the bough and making a snatch with the other hand, deeper into the elegant foliage of the *leptomeria*.

Her grip holds. The savage traction threatening to tear her head from her shoulders eases along with the tautness of the overhead cable. But, the unbearable pressure in her head and agony of her throat remain as the noose begrudges any loosening of its hold.

She concentrates on holding her breath as she snatches one hand after another, deeper and deeper into the shrub. At last, with titanic effort, she finds the traction of a foot on the coarse bark of the bough and stands upright once more. She releases one hand from the *leptomeria* and gouges her fingers into the softness of her throat until, at last, she is able to rip back the strangling grip of the noose.

Coughing and gagging on foliage and fruit that have sprayed into her mouth during the struggle, she almost falls again before she gets the loop back over her head. She lets go of the cable and it swings away as she drops to the ground, lying in a daze for perhaps a minute, perhaps an hour.

Eventually, she stands, shifting uncomfortably. She slides off her trousers, eases the vile underpants free and weighs them for a moment, as if collecting data. How heavy they seem. She flings them away and re-dresses.

Her throat burns, her neck is a vice. There is a jackhammer in her head and all the muscles in her shoulders are torn or strained. Leaving the cord hanging, she walks back to the road like a zombie. There's a tourist car bumping along the corrugations, bound for the lookout, so she hides behind a log until it's gone. Then she begins the interminable trudge, a kilometre back to the house. She thinks no more about plants or ants. All there is, is the matter of the foetal cord blood: the facts of her betrayal play over and over in her mind. She will make them pay!

She's grateful now the husband has gone. She couldn't let him see her like this. Avoiding the mirror, she rifles the vanity for pain relief. Make-up, scissors and small brushes clatter to the floor. There is extra-strength codeine but she stays her hand: the meeting! She's damned now if she won't go, but she can't be groggy. With a palmful of paracetamol, disprin and brufen, she pours a glass of water and leans against the shower, bracing against the small hell of swallowing. Her throat is a gag and fights the pills to the last.

The pain, so exquisite around her delicate throat, turns brutal as it radiates through her upper body, binding and stabbing. A basal headache pounds to the rhythm of her heart and she tries touching her scalp, curious why it's numb, but winces at the effort and slowly lowers her hand. Everything above her scapulas feels fused and the shower is purgatory, lifting limbs, leaning this way and that as she struggles to scrub herself. Once cleansed, she feels returned to the margins of the world. She tells herself, twenty-five minutes to be out the door, but can't believe it.

Forgoing the towel, she walks out and sits on the bed. The suit she selected last night is still there and she reaches to put it on but finds herself unable to lean forward. So she sits there, streaming water onto the covers, feeling the part of herself she despises most on the verge of tears. How could they do it? The documents. No, they can go to hell.

This reminds her of the cocaine her husband thinks he keeps hidden in the back of his underwear drawer. Pondering the binary orbit of cunning and stupidity that is man, she slides her bottom off the bed and groans to her feet, retrieves a key from inside a pair of socks in her own drawer, shuffles down the hall and unlocks his room. The coke's still there, next to the documents she found last night. Back in her room, the key is handy to dip and snort and the sneeze almost floors her, the pain a bewilderment, ears ringing. But she braces herself again and gives the other nostril a dose, this time without a sneeze. Things are coming into focus. The pain remains but it's losing its grip. She goes back to the black suit, picks off a piece or two of lint and gets on with the job of dressing for a meeting with the minister. Someone will swing today.

The drive down the hill gives her time to collect her thoughts but she has to battle to deconstruct her anger. There'll be the Health Minister, which means the department head, Dal Eckhardt, will be there too. The Dalek. She rails at having to put up with a former psych nurse as Director General of Health. But he's untouchable, so she leashes her thoughts away from union mates and party politics, takes a deep breath and drops one hand off the wheel to ease the nag in her shoulder. They'll be expecting Pete to do the dirty work. She lifts the free hand to correct her hair and winces... Pete!

Professor Peter Picault is her boss and dearest, only friend. Director of the Hovel Area Health Service, she knows it's him who'll put the pickaxe in. What do they expect, she wonders; she's stripped her hospitals, closed her theatres, reduced staff by twenty-five per cent. Christ, she's got one IC unit left to cover half a region! Who else would've had the guts to be so resented, to keep on coming! It's what they wanted from her. She thinks how her single-mindedness has saved them millions, of the toll it takes every day to run a crammed system at crisis level. Now they find themselves unpopular, they want a scapegoat?

And Pete, how could he? She should have known not to trust him; he might hold a public position as regional director, but he rarely mentions being an executive member on the Council of Surgeons. She shifts in her seat and blares the horn at a stop-go woman trying to halt traffic at the roadworks.

Pete doles out the pittance Eckhardt drops down to him like it was coming out of his own pocket. 'My dear, you hospital managers are beggars for punishment,' he'd said, laughing over lunch one day. 'You've got no cartel, no self-regulated short supply. Look, I envy you not having to worry about Bayswater traffic, but try to understand: the punters want local public hospitals, but we want fully insured, private patients, prepared to travel between integrated clinics. Our clinics. And, actually, our model is the one the minister prefers.'

Is that why he put a vampire in charge of his blood bank, she'd almost joked.

Cautious to slow down at the speed camera, she cruises impatiently for two hundred metres and then floors it, reaching a hand out to steady the briefcase on the other seat.

Her iPhone buzzes. It's him, getting back about a query she'd forwarded before leaving home. Yes, he, Pete'll be there. The minister, Eckhardt too. Of course there'll be a minutes secretary and, oh yes, Sally Winter from the Professional Ethics and Conduct Unit. No good morning, no how are you. Only silence on the cord blood issue. She'd known it all along, PECU, the gestapo, they were going to take her down! And Sally Winter, she thinks, where do they dig them up?

Pulling in to the hospital grounds where the meeting's due in five minutes, there's an ambulance hurtling through the roundabout with its beacons on. She has to swerve out of its way. By habit, she peers at the windscreen as it passes, trying to see if it's him, the whistle-blower who took the cord blood issue to the media. Why don't people just do their job? Path labs pay good money for cord blood. Well, some path labs do: it's a delicate substance and a delicate issue, parental consent being the constraint it is these days. But Jesus, where do people think the money comes from when they need a paediatrician? Out of a budget like Pete's?

She can't make out the faces of the paramedics behind the glare of their windscreen. No, you need a reliable, impromptu courier to get a highly perishable product like cord blood to its buyer, out of hours, below the radar. Someone who'll run fast and silent, take their cash and go. You should be able to pay them from the neck down.

She watches the ambulance swing out of the roundabout and accelerate away under its strobes. The car behind her honks its horn.

'Sally Winter returned, and you've changed your hair,' she says, holding Sally in a gaze that flushes the skin across the top of the young woman's chest. She'd heard that Sal had taken a promotion and moved back from Mid Coast Region. It's surprising she'd had the nerve but, with word out the old witch was on trial, she'd probably hoped to get back in time for a burning.

'Hello, Glenda, how nice to see you,' she replies unconvincingly, watching with suspicion as the older woman brings a chair over. 'What's happened to your voice?'

The minister's in a huddle with the Dalek and doesn't look up as Glenda rearranges the seat. Pete's the last one through the door and she ignores him. What she does is sit close to the younger woman and, under the table, move a foot up against Sally's. She jumps and snatches her foot away but Glenda can smell her discomfort. Always a gamey kind of girl, Sal.

Glenda fights a pain threshold to pivot her head with nonchalance, lightly adjusting the scarf covering the weals on her throat, fixing the young woman's eye with bird-like acuity. Her smile is a display of teeth as she says, 'So, my dear, how's the husband? Still with the church?'

The emotion that plays momentarily across Winter's face is unreadable but tiny beads of sweat begin to pill on her upper lip. Her smell becomes stronger, sharper. She says nothing, just turns back to her papers and shuffles them as if they hadn't been in order. There's a comforting drip in Glenda's throat from the top-up of cocaine she's had before the meeting. It's taking the edge off risk as well as pain. With nothing left to lose, she watches Sally move, breathing her in.

A young woman with Sal's looks might carry around a burden of surprise and disappointment about what people really want from her life, and what they'll do and say to get it. But it was Sal herself who had been the surprise. Glenda still had all of her love letters. Even the last ones, so touching, so comical in the denunciation of her husband: 'If you'll just wait a few years, till the children are grown, I'll leave him then and we can be together forever.'

It was a naivety that had been all too easy to manipulate. In the end, the husband thought they'd moved away because he'd put his foot down and demanded it. Are they all so stupid?

But what Sal really resented was how she'd come to be blackmailed. 'Look,' Glenda had explained, 'you're well up in PECU, I've got problems with your lot investigating my lot's triage statistics, this is hard for me too, but I'm the one who'll wear it. Honestly, I've got no choice, I have to insist you help me out!'

The girl shouldn't have taken it personally. Whatever, she complied, the investigation got nobbled and Sal got bent.

'It's so good to see you too,' Glenda murmurs, turning away, reaching into her briefcase.

Sally Walker gives no indication of having heard.

The Dalek clears his throat and opens the meeting, being as curt as an apparatchik can be. They must be in a hurry. It's hard to focus, with cocaine converting the insufferable drone of his words into birdsong. She watches the dart of his prominent Adam's apple, his bulging eyes, and thinks how like an emu he is. The eyes never stray towards her as he hrooms and thrums into a mind-numbing rhythm of jargon about Key Performance Indicators and Patient Journeys, settling into a dissertation despite the initial haste.

The minister drums his fingers. He looks short of patience, like he wants to journey elsewhere. She observes the absence of rapport between the two men, recognising the resentment ministers always feel when their party machine parachutes its creature in to head the department.

The Dalek fires a few procedural questions at Pete, but Pete's ahead of him, with all the right answers to hand.

Glenda starts to lose track, her mind yawing off course and splintering against the documents under her hand. Why had he hidden them? Does he hate her so much? What is she without this job? She looks up at Pete and hatred wells from the dark places of her soul.

Warming up, Eckhardt wants to drone on about some new superclinic integration initiatives when the minister cuts him off.

'Yes, thanks, Dal, very succinct. Now,' looking at his watch, 'Peter, we have an unfortunate matter scheduled for today's agenda and I'd like you to give us a précis and action plan about how you're dealing with it.' Still without a glance towards Glenda, he continues, 'It's a shame when things like this get into the media, but Health, more than any other corporate body, has a duty of disclosure that is requisite to the level of trust the public requires from us.'

It dawns on Glenda, he's practising lines for a radio interview where he plans to display her severed head. That's what the clock watching's about.

Pete leaps to his feet, eager to please. She takes hold of her papers as she watches him work into his subject. Long ago, she'd flattered him shamelessly about the cosmetic surgery he'd had done. Now, watching his oversized lips labouring, waiting for the fixed arch of his eyebrows to actually mean something, she wonders why she ever admired him. She'd accepted as an expression of natural order how he'd recognised her talents and promoted her accordingly.

For years they've been a hardball team, sharing what they did together because they know the real world and what has to be done. People had been dealt with ruthlessly, but only for the sake of efficiency. They had no right to complain; people are no better than the position they fill. And, if their position has to go, it does. But she, Glenda, has given so much to this team, left so much behind – friends, Sal, a marriage it would seem – all for the sake of a job that has become her life.

At last, he says the words 'foetal cord blood' and every eye in the room swivels onto her as if someone has pulled away a dust sheet. He pauses for effect, raising a hand for emphasis. It's time.

She stands and holds the papers as high as her pains allow, watching the eyes follow. 'Thanks, Professor. Minister, I have to add this material to the record.'

Even the minutes secretary looks up, though Pete's arm stays suspended as if he's conjured something unexpected. No one thought the dead would speak, and she moves fast.

'Minister, the path lab that bought the cord blood solicited the sale. These documents show who owns the lab. He owns it.'

She's pointing with her free hand at the professor and his lips are spluttering in protest, his expression an involuntary mask, smooth and hard as a carp's face. He lowers his arm in increments, thrown by the reversal of circumstances.

Eckhardt peers gormlessly through the hubbub, down to his own briefing papers, up to Pete and back down again. The minister's eyes are bulging as he stares across at Eckhardt, and it's not a pretty sight. Sally's face is a pale shape to the left and Glenda wishes she could turn to it. But there's no time.

She turns to the minute taker whose pen has paused and says, 'Madam Secretary, I want the minutes taped onto audio from here…'

At this point, the minister's voice cuts across her. 'Yeah, look, Glenda, I'm sure that won't be necessary. Just give us a summary of what you've got. Quickly.'

She turns and measures him eye to eye, pausing for effect, thinking that the dubious advantage of marriage to a senior detective lies in the politic of his job: the people who owe him, private investigators, federal policemen. Pete was clever; he'd never talked up the cash value of cord blood. He'd always discussed it as if its value was solely as a key to stem cell research. He'd never even dropped the name of the one path lab buying unaccredited cord blood into the same conversation as the blood itself. But was he so stupid to think his wife couldn't be tracked as the beneficiary of the trust set up to own the pathology franchise?

What had it all been for, all the years of slow estrangement from her husband as she poured her life into her office, into the gilded old man opposite her now? The gradual disappearance of children-that-never-were from conversations that slowly dried up and blew away. Even the odd illicit pleasure, like Sal, that she'd stolen from office sidelines, why did they mean nothing compared to a job that has brought her so low?

She fights back a sob. She wants to shout the truth at these people, that she hadn't kept the money, that she did it out of desperation, to keep her hospitals afloat. But there's no point. The truth is nothing other than what you make of it. Everyone in the room knows this one fact. They wouldn't be here otherwise. So she ignores the tear that splashes onto the table in front of her and forges ahead while Pete is still gaping at the papers in her hand.

She tables the documents and explains the trail of evidence her husband was meant to dig up on her behalf. The trail in the papers she found last night, hidden like a parting insult, in an underwear drawer. There were triplicate copies, something that once would have made her laugh at policeman's habits. She tosses one across to the minister, and Eckhardt has to lean across his table to share a view.

She had been going to give one to Pete, but changes her mind and hands it over to Sal instead. With the heat off her, she sees the girl looking cool enough to appreciate a change in the wind. Glenda looks down at her and feels listless and alone.

Pete rallies. He gabbles evasively how he'd no idea about the ownership provisions of his wife's trust and, really, it's not an issue that should be allowed to interrupt the good governance of the current meeting. It all rings hollow.

The minister is rolling his eyes and reaching for his phone. He'd have a radio interview to cancel, so she forces herself to seize the initiative and interrupt again.

'Minister, good governance is the issue, especially how it'll be reported by the media if this gets out. I've been lured into this situation by a corrupt supervisor and I'm damned if I won't see the matter dealt with, one way or the other.'

Picault is trying to protest again but she raises her voice and shouts him down. He slams his fist on the table and shakes his head but she holds the minister's eyes as she continues. 'The professor's contract is up soon and I can't work with him. So frankly, minister, if it's him or me, spare a thought about the media implications!'

Picault is clambering around his table but his movements intercept the fury that Glenda has raised in the minister's eye. It stops Pete dead and he stammers again for words. The minister looks back to his phone and his knuckles are wrapped around it, white. He snaps it shut, puts it in his pocket and takes a deep breath.

Glenda drives on fast. 'You need an independent review of this. It doesn't have to be formally minuted. We've got Sally Winter from PECU. She can give us a legal overview here and now.' Glenda collapses back into her seat. She doesn't look at Sally and keeps her foot to herself. Which way will she jump? Where does she think her bed is made these days?

Picault is standing in front of his table, looking wrong footed in the sudden silence. He runs a hand through his silver mane, then holds it up as if he was stopping traffic.

Eckhardt hisses, 'Just shut up and let the minister think.'

The minister wishes he could sack everyone in the room. He's already got shock jocks and tabloid hacks on his back, baying for blood about this foetal cord issue. God, they'll be calling it Vampiregate if it isn't contained. Picault's seat on the Council of Surgeons makes him hard to get rid of. But the council's not going to want to see a ballooning scandal either. Hostile scrutiny of health care reforms that transfer taxpayer funds into privately owned for-profit clinics is the last thing the surgeons will want. Picault's stupidity, if exposed, could be a PR disaster for the whole reform agenda. Still, he thinks, how can I dump a workhorse like Picault at the demand of a little piece of work like this Glenda? I don't like her and don't trust her, but God, he thinks, I've got fifteen minutes to sort this mess out and only a moron like Eckhardt to do it with.

Exasperated, he looks at Sally Winter and says, 'Okay, you, what do you think?'

Sally flowers into the occasion like a rose. She stands, revealing her impressive height. Her arguments against the professor gleam with the dew of common sense yet tumble out of a snappy, open and shut case. She mitigates Glenda's situation with an overview that is stern yet compassionate.

Glenda watches the minister watching the girl with a sudden interest she understands only too well. Tired, she feels a sense of gladness for Sally, as if the younger woman wasn't just another rat off a sinking ship. She knows it's the last ghost of the cocaine, but she feels a memory of the weight of Sally pass down through her arms and move away, beyond her fingers, beyond reach. She shivers. She looks at her hand and it's shaking.

The minister has started nodding in sync with Sally's points and there seems little doubt about the way he'll jump. Glenda shudders one last time as her exhaustion turns. Cynicism creeps across her like unwelcome hands. She feels suffocated in this room of lies. Like a tape recording that had to be played, she hears Sally launching into a discourse outlining the proprieties of refilling the professor's lapsing contract with Glenda herself.

It's too much, even for Glenda, and she's thinking what a bad actor the girl has become after all, when she sees both the minister and Eckhardt nodding in unison. Pete is packing his briefcase. It's all become a dream, a vortex, and she has to get out before it sucks her down. She has an urgent need to find fresh air, to breathe deep and recharge herself.

She staggers to her feet. 'Look,' she interjects, 'I've come here feeling very unwell. I don't want to upset these deliberations but I think now it might be influenza.' She indicates her throat. 'That means I'm obliged by departmental guidelines to leave the room. Unless you all want to put on surgical masks.'

Minister and Dalek turn their faces towards her but maintain a synchronicity of benevolent nods. Pete slams his case shut and swings it down from the table, shifting sideways in his seat.

Glenda takes a last look into Sally Winter's face. Sal has turned towards her and is looking down from her height. Glenda expects to see a play of saccharine-coated hatred or the false bonhomie of a wink, but all she sees is kindness and concern. It comes like a blow. The young woman reaches out a hand that touches Glenda's arm slightly, gently. Strands of hair obscure one of Sally's eyes, but a gleam of moisture is visible in the other. The postural shift of her gesture rotates a reflection of Glenda onto the cornea of Sally's clear eye. Glenda wishes that she could reach across and move the strands of hair. But the impossibility of the gesture makes the older woman reel within a sudden disjuncture of time and place. She pulls free and heads for the door, grabbing the jamb for support as she passes from the room.

Outside in the clear air, composed again after another top-up, she sees the ambulance bay in a state of gridlock. There are eight wagons waiting to unload, half of them yet to be triaged. She pauses, wanting to leave, but the regional ambulance superintendent is marching out of Casualty, obviously disgruntled at his inability to relieve his crews.

She knows that a second file in her briefcase holds a summary of clinical errors the whistle-blower has made in the months since his revelations. It took many lonely hours to collate this information, searching through the hospital copy of every single ambulance case sheet, looking for his name as compiler, comparing the treatments he'd given to his compulsory protocols.

It turns out he's a hopeless paramedic, probably stressed out like the rest of them. Probably more so given his whistle-blowing tendencies. He'd be right on the edge. She's kept the list handy for an occasion like this. Weary as she is, the opportunity for a chat with the superintendent can't be overlooked. It's her job.

A few potato chips lie strewn on the concrete as she walks over. Some mynah birds are squabbling over them when a currawong swoops down like a pirate and dispossesses them of their feast. Glenda looks at the black bird as she approaches. The thing she admires about currawongs is the depth in their eyes, that deep yellow gaze. It's like looking through time, right back into the eye of a miniature, predatory dinosaur. The bird crouches over its spoils and watches keenly as she walks past. Then, dropping a chip from its beak, it lopes along behind.

Dewey Street

The flats in Dewey Street have a bad reputation. Two skinny girls cry in a doorway as the ambulance pulls up.

The tattooed man behind them shouts, 'Hurry, just fucken hurry.'

Inside, they find a young man dead. Late teens, pulseless, still warm.

Geoff lifts a hand and lets it flop. The pupils are pinpoint. A heavy blanket is thrown aside and they drag the body down from lounge to stinking carpet.

The tattooed man frowns as the girls say, 'Bin down here two hours by himself. We been upstairs, watchin' telly.'

Track marks obvious, needle missing, girls admit it was heroin. Tattoo clenches his fists and leaves the room. There's a wail as Geoff rips open the boy's shirt and he is surprised to hear a calm voice ask the girls to wait outside, his own voice. They should have been at school.

Geoff's mate Len's quick with the defib pads and the machine beeps into life as a third entity, waiting command, recording. Geoff looks at Len, who is lean and muscular, and wonders for a moment why he thinks of him as an older man. Yesterday was the first day they'd worked together as, having been with the service for less than a month, Len is still a probationer, a fact that hangs on Geoff like the fug of the room. He brushes the dead boy's eyelashes one last time, wishing they would flicker, and commits.

It's his second day back at work. No one had said that he was suspended from duty, just that he shouldn't come back until the court case was done. All that time alone with what had happened, twelve weeks for the coroner to hand down her findings. Paranoid in the witness stand, Geoff had explained away his actions by turning every inconvenient fact back on his employer. He left the stand expecting a reckoning.

Yesterday they'd been dragged far from station, flogged through one squalid drama after another across every undesirable suburb of the city. Four hours of unwanted overtime that he'd railed against over the radio, making a fool of himself, radio control riding unperturbed over his every protest, handing down job after job. Whether or not they were the closest wagon had made no difference.

Here, now, with every second counting, the machine displays the patient's flat line like an accusation, recording for later examination everything that Geoff does or does not do about it. Lowering a knee onto the congealed shag pile, he forgets about Len, the court, and sees only a dead boy.

Len starts to sweat. It makes him worry that Geoff might smell last night's stale booze. He was a paramedic in New Zealand before moving across the ditch, but prefers to keep that fact to himself. No one expects too much from a probationer, which is a relief. You carry things, pass them, keep your mouth shut. But he dials up paddles on the defibrillator out of habit, pausing his fingers at the sight of the flat line, saying, 'Asystole, Geoff, no shock.' Leaving the machine, he pushes the drug kit closer to his partner and begins cardiac massage.

Geoff is trying to slide a tube down the boy's throat but lubricant makes his gloves slip as he grips the tongue to move it to one side. The boy's lips are cracked, freckles on his cheeks, eyes half-shut as if resigned to this one last indignity. After a struggle, Geoff seats the tube neatly over the larynx before fumbling with a big syringe to inflate the tube's plastic cup and so isolate the airway. Then he trims the whole arrangement tight with a cord around the boy's neck and tests for air entry. Lungs rise with each squeeze of the resus bag. They're in business.

Asystole, thinks Geoff. Okay, adrenalin. Engorged in death, a fat jugular stands out on the boy's throat, promising a shortcut to drop the drug straight into his heart. Geoff swabs the throat and pierces the plump line of the vein with the razor tip of a large-bore cannula. Len is keeping count with the compressions and reaches across a couple of times to squeeze the resus bag when Geoff forgets. Geoff mutters when no flashback of blood appears in the hub of the cannula to prove it has gone home. With every second counting, his hand hovers uncertain, then pulls the cannula back out and dumps it in the bin. 'Blown it,' he mutters as blood wells dark and slow from the wound.

Len takes over the bag as well as the compressions and his mate shifts to crouch above an arm, rotating the elbow through dingy light, looking for the shadow of a vein. But even through the gloom it's plain that the boy's ravaged blood vessels are useless.

Geoff shouts out for the girls to hit the light and a flea jumps startled as he spots another maybe vein in the forearm. A tourniquet and Len's exertions bring it up.

Time crawls, Geoff fumbles for a new pin, ratting for the bung to go with it, the wrappings, so stubborn. Cinch the tourniquet tighter, another swab and again he's ready. And again, the needle goes in sweet but shows no flashback.

The flow of the job is falling apart and Geoff has a sudden sense of déjà vu, imagining himself jump up and run from the room. Len senses his uncertainty and is about to remind him that radio control promised them a back-up car when there's a noise at the door and the weeping girls part.

A woman with heavy make-up and an over-tight uniform strides into the room, lugging a big kit. Her head tilts bird-like to one side as she falsettos, 'Geoff, how ya goin', luvvy? Whatta we got?'

Emma's been in the job as many years as Geoff, plus a few. Her blusher and waistline have thickened, but her mind is as nimble as ever. The sharps container on her kit rattles as she drops it to the floor. Geoff holds a discreet hand above the blown cannula and gives her a studied recital of events, the feigned casualness of which makes Len look away. He cracks a bit at the end, though, explaining his embarrassment about being unable to obtain intravenous access, at last moving his hand aside to reveal the second failure.

'Oh, you got the tube down his throat, though, luvvy,' she says and, glancing over Len's continuing efforts, trills, 'You boys have done really well.'

Geoff restrains a show of gratitude and takes back the ventilation bag from Len, who is dripping from the heat of the room and the exertions of cardiac massage. Emma flicks through their kit for another cannula and an adrenalin packet which she snaps open. She takes the ventilation bag from Geoff's hand, unplugs the tube to the boy's throat and jets the adrenalin straight into his lungs. Geoff takes the bag back from her and turns his gaze to the defibrillator screen, watching for any quivers on the flat line that they might now shock. Nothing. She's already stepping over the prostrate body and crouching, needle in hand, above the other ravaged arm.

She'd always been intimidating in a way, her once-youthful good looks caked hard under unnecessary make-up, the quaint distraction of her 'luvvies' and 'dearies' amusing but a non sequitur. Geoff had never seen her fail to deal decisively with any situation. Glancing at her lining up the pin, he remembers the one occasion he'd seen her look distressed, many years before at a cot death. The baby's lungs had been so tight they couldn't be inflated with a bag mask, Emma had tried to give it mouth to mouth but been rebuked by a senior clinician. He'd seen her close to tears then, holding them back in anger.

Len switches his gaze between the pair: they say so little and the only noise in the overheated room is the squelch of the resus bag and a matching gurgle from the patient's lungs. He follows Geoff's gaze back to the screen and ventures 'No change' to break the silence, to remind them of his presence.

'Lungs are congested…' says Geoff by way of reply.

'Would've aspirated before you got here, poor thing,' finishes Emma, studying the entry point of her own cannula. She shifts it in and out, a little to either side, looks up to Len and says, 'How 'bout you get those girls to write down some patient details, luvvy.' Then, to Geoff, 'Can't get this one either. Was sure I was in.' She pulls the pin clear, leans carefully past Len and drops it into the sharps box, taping a wad of gauze over a slow red bead.

Len finds himself relieved to be tasked. He goes over a mental check list of questions to ask the sentinels at the door, but again they part and two more paramedics enter the room.

A tall, ungainly woman cranes to look over the head of her slight companion, as if taking an inventory, then disappears back out the door. The shorter woman, a smudged tattoo half-visible on her biceps, regards the kneeling trio with the slow sweep of one visible eye, weighing them, the dead boy and all the contents of the room with an equal dispassion. 'Yeah?' she says.

The three have paused, all looking up at the slender woman.

Geoff wants to reply, to start at the start and justify himself. 'Dell…' he manages to say before Emma cuts him off, explaining succinctly that the patient's persistent asystole has not yet responded to the ten millilitres of one in ten thousand adrenalin she has administered via Geoff's airway tube.

Again it all sounds too casual, though Len notices that the undusted skin around the base of Emma's neck has flushed bright red.

Dell gives a slight nod and steps around the axis of the body until she's next to Len. She touches his shoulder and murmurs, 'Keep going, mate,' as she follows the glazing line of sight from the dead boy's eyes, past the bleeding neck and Len's redoubled efforts, down, to the punctures on the arms. 'Cant get a line in?' she asks rhetorically.

Emma shifts as Dell descends to join them in their crouch.

Dell moves her one lock of dependent hair away from the eye it obscures, anchoring it expertly behind an ear. Then, picking up a hand, she probes the quick of a fingernail to see its colour shift when she presses. Still solacing the hand, she looks around the room once more, at the blankets, the heater purring in the corner. 'No wonder you got no flashback,' she says, lowering the hand gently. 'He's started to coagulate. He's only warm as this because of the environment.'

The tall woman comes bustling back into the room, wrestling with an awkward carry-board that knocks a jagged chip off the door jamb.

'Nah,' says Dell, 'you can take that back to the wagon.'

Her partner pivots with a studiously blank face and a dangerous swing of the board, then bumps her way back out.

Emma's and Geoff's eyes meet and both see a kind of relief, a burden of responsibility lifted. They stand wordlessly and turn away. Dell is already at the door, leading the girls outside, murmuring words of comfort. Len has tunnel vision. Trying to formulate questions for the girls, he's missed the import of Dell's pronouncement and still hopes to see the job resolved in the patient's favour. Continuing with his chest compressions, he sees Geoff unplug the defibrillator and Emma lift her kit.

Geoff turns to him and says, 'Len, just leave it, mate, leave it for the cops.'

It, thinks Len. It?

Outside, the last of the winter sun steps weak off the apex of a cypress pine and huddles in some chimney smoke. Emma walks up to Geoff as he stows his gear through the side door. Like a ritual, they express their disappointment at the fate of the patient and agree about the waste of such a young life. A truth they both intend to turn their backs on and forget, like so many others.

Dell has reluctantly passed the girls on to some coppers and walks over. The pair attempt to engage her in their conversation and ask about the triathlon everyone had heard she'd won. But the hair has fallen back across Dell's eye and she looks uneasy with their small talk. She drifts away to her car and the paperwork.

The chill descends and Emma zips her jacket. Geoff looks at his watch. He should have been on his way home twenty minutes ago and still hasn't started his own case sheet. There's an awkward silence before Emma speaks in a lower voice than normal, saying she'd followed the progress of the coroner's case. She's glad to see Geoff back. It was sad what happened, but a person can only do what they can. Her gaze shifts focus into the back of the ambulance as she speaks. He swivels but there's nothing there. When he turns back, Emma has fished a tissue out of her pocket and is correcting a smudge on her mascara. She puts a hand to Geoff's elbow, walks back to her car.

Geoff climbs onto his seat and picks up the case sheet folder, holding it on his lap, unopened. Len is there at the wheel and looks across at him, about to speak. But the call sign of their car comes over the radio so he picks up the mike instead and replies. Control tells them that they are required for a possible fractured hip in the next suburb and Geoff looks down to the folder, his mouth a taut line.

Dell and her mate are still parked across the road. She hears the job go down and does a quick data analysis, factoring her own need for extra overtime pay against the possibility of yet more aggro from the ex when she goes to get the kids. Vectoring into consideration Geoff's obvious distress at his involuntary overtime the evening before, she picks up the mike and announces flat that her car will be doing the job. Taken short, the controller acquiesces and reroutes the case. With her partner staring daggers at her, Dell leans forward and activates the strobes. Geoff watches them cruise up the hill to the intersection, glide to a momentary halt then turn into the gloom before the lights flick green.

Harmonic

The bitch is stealthy, prick-ears lowered, moving smoothly forward in a crouch. She flushes a tawny grassbird out of its yellow stalks and the chase begins. Across the hillside, out of sight in the gully, up the opposing slope and back around the upper basin.

He watches bemused, understanding the dog's desire to chase, wondering why the grass bird doesn't fly above the reach of her jaws. The bird appears to court danger, flitting low and letting the bitch close in. Across the distance he hears her jaws snap shut as she leaps. But the bird has jagged effortlessly aside and set a new tangent for the pursuit that soon has the bitch's tongue lolling. Her yelping and yowling grows ragged as she tires and he raises his voice to call her back, wondering if she really wants to kill that bird, and if the grassbird enjoys giving her the run-around.

She responds to command, throwing herself against his legs in a final check of her momentum. He steadies himself with effort and she's sitting on his foot and leaning up against him, smelling of fresh straw, looking back with a face that has to be laughing. He wants to stoop and smooth away grass seeds, lay hands on her steam-engine pant. But he knows better than to try.

He looks back to the house. Denise'll be home from work soon and she won't be happy about his outing. Better start the long limp back. And, he tells himself wincing, stop thinking about the Endone.

Top gate's visible in the distance and he keeps an eye on it in case he has to hurry. He doesn't want another piece of her mind. Each footfall is a jolt that ratchets pain, tightening ache into spasm. The old kurrajong is a haven of shade and he leans against it for a moment. It doesn't help. His slow progress turns the bitch's orbit into an ellipse as she scouts ahead then scoots back in a close pass of his heels. He leans gratefully on the house gate before fidgeting with the sticky latch. Guess, after all this time, she'll have to get someone else to fix it. Inside, the shade is luxury and the lounge is broad. But he makes for the packet on top of the fridge and breaks out a tablet and then, what the hell, another.

He's groggy when he wakes. The bloody leatherheads are going crazy fighting each other in the callistemon outside his window and he raps the pane with one fist but it doesn't stop their brawling. He hears that one has detached itself from the melee and begun working through the complicated chords of its song. A glance out the window reveals its tail hanging down from the gutter, moving to the rhythm of the music. One note sounds like it's being harmonised by a second songster but he knows from past experience that the singer will be alone.

He tries to memorise the bird's scale in order to predict the harmonic note, but can't do it. Bloody birdbrain's got me mesmerised he thinks, rolling his legs out from under the sheet, sitting slowly up in a tender manoeuvre. His dependent legs are stick thin and yellow. He looks at them across the great, taut bulge of his belly and finds the sight disgusting.

Denise has headed off to work already and he's glad. Solitude. Well, almost, he thinks looking at the top of the fridge – God, is that a rat gnawing at my guts – Denise's got another packet in from the chemist.

She'd cried again last night, said damn you, Geoff, I'm staying home. Look at you, luv. How the hell do you think I can leave you like this every day?

Don't worry yourself, he'd replied sourly. I just wanna be alone. He'd almost added that, soon enough, she'd get to make all his bloody decisions for him anyway. But he'd caught himself in time. He wonders why he's mean to her when all she can do is take it. She's the most decent person that he knows, but she's got to get used to the facts.

He brushes away a tear that's got nothing to do with sorrow. They're there all the time. Wipes the back of his hand on his boxer shorts, wondering where the hell his emotions went. Sits down on the lounge, keeling slowly back in pain and looking up at the rafters. Jesus, the curve in 'em, never did put those bloody collar ties up. I'll make a note of it for Denise. She'll have to get some bastard in to do it before the whole roof sags.

There's a bump at the door. The bitch has heard him moving. He's got to empty his bag anyway so he groans to his feet and opens the door. She strolls in like she owns the place and sprawls on the floor with a groan of her own, one that morphs into a contented sigh. He looks into her eye and it stares straight back, yellow. That makes two of us, he thinks, as he moves to the sink so his jaundiced hand can run some water for the coffee he hopes will clear his mind. Then he stumps off down the hallway to take care of the bag.

The coffee's scalding but he lies down out of habit to sip and the ascites has domed his belly taut, but he manages, stubborn. He'd planned to put enough painkillers aside for the overdose. When the time was right. A pipe dream, he thinks now, watching the sun shaft through the leadlight and illuminate the rendered wall with red and blue and green. God, how he needs those pills. If only they wouldn't muddle his thoughts. It's like looking down a tunnel. He sets the coffee aside, dozes.

The frog that wakes him is calling excitedly from the downpipe, predicting rain. Good news at last, he thinks, rousing himself to a doorway where the harsh day declares itself. But the sky is cloudless and the only movement on the drought-parched paddock is a willy-willy churning grass stalks and dust along the curve of its touchdown. There's no frog chirruping in the gutter. It must have been a dream. He sits down at the table to watch the willy-willy die, takes another Endone.

That's it, he thinks: like looking down a tunnel. Your life goes round and round. You don't stay still, just get older, spiral into it. When you look back at what you've done, you're looking down the inside of a spiral. He snorts with amusement at the philosophy of his thoughts.

The willy-willy drops its last thread of grass as it lifts back up into the eddy from which it came. Denise'd love this, he thinks, the great Himself converted to an air sign at last. No. His life was heavy, always was. A bastard of a thing. He hates religion, remembers the nuns who beat it into him: mad old psychos ranting about hell, twisted. The beatings, they could barely control themselves. No, fuck them and their god.

But twisted out of what? Where does it all begin? He remembers his mother and knows that in his case he came into the world out of love, he can be sure of that much. Looks down and the dog's moved up and put its head on his knee, gazing up at him. He brushes away another one of the persistent tears and the dog tries to lick at it. He pushes the bitch away. But you die alone. Everyone. Seen it himself often enough.

That evening he makes an effort to eat a couple of mouthfuls of the dinner she's cooked. She's marinated the chicken and it would have been his favourite, once. He can see her looking at him surreptitiously over her plate, sees the effort it's costing her to hold her tongue. And in the silence he's grateful.

It was a long night, interminable and not over with first light and the cackle and strife outside in the callistemon. He'd tried taking a second sleeping pill as well as the pain relief and might have dozed for an hour. She'd looked in after six but he'd pretended to be asleep and stirred just enough so she'd know he hadn't popped his clogs. Just leave, he thinks, hearing her linger outside the door; just go to work.

Outside at last, the air is still. The usual cloud of house swallows has wheeled away for the day. He walks around to the hose and shoos the brawling leatherheads from the callistemon. They move to the willow to smooth their feathers and smoulder, watching him out of dark-blood eyes, black lit red, smouldering at him. He gives them the finger and gets on with the watering.

If anything makes him sad, it's the drought. He tries not to look out into the paddock. The well is still holding up and so he keeps water up to the trees and shrubs of the house yard. The place has become an oasis for migrating birds and sometimes he loses himself in the fragile grace of wrens and thornbills, dancing in his yard. One day last week a flock of zebra finches had poured through the fence and disappeared into the dry grass like a torrent, sifting and flitting away through the sour, unkempt stalks.

But not today. Only stillness. The heat of the day is building and even the friarbirds are taking time in the willow to relax their feathers and loll their leather heads. Then he hears the flute. From the veranda, a harmony so haunting that he twists off the nozzle and turns. The pied butcherbird that sits on the handrail has its head raised, lost in the rapture of its own melody. The man stands as still as the sun to listen.

One lone thornbill breaks cover in the bay tree, edging forward as if mesmerised, and the butcherbird pounces, arcing across the gap, fluttering back to the handrail encumbered, bashing the tiny bird against hardwood. With one foot on the stunned thornbill, the butcherbird begins to tear away its feathers, throwing them nonchalantly towards the spectator. He moves forward enraged but the butcherbird darts away with its meal, drifting bloody feathers as it cuts a flat trajectory towards the distant apple gum.

The silence resumes, broken only by the rattle-and-thwack from an old plastic flowerpot that the bitch has started to toss and chase. The first hint of a breeze breathes in from the south-west and he watches it catch the slipstream of feathers and spin them away, across the paddock. He drops the hose, winces up the steps and makes his way into the cool seclusion of the house.

All his life, he's just got on with it. Never much wasted time looking back was how he saw it. But now, you can't face up to the future you don't have. Can't come to grips with that. And the more he thinks about it, the more he realises, that's not how it was anyway: talk about seize the day; he'd always figured, why stop there? Reach right through and grab the future. Or what you can get of it. The future, what a joke! A wish list you've already made up, a grab-bag of desires. It seems to him that, whatever he's really been facing up to, he's had his back turned to the future. Because the things he'd been groping for had come out of his past, spin-offs of preconception and want.

He shuts his eyes and takes a breath, hears its wheeze, a thrum in his chest.

Paused inside these walls and panes, he can feel the moment of his life decay. If the tunnel of his past had a particular turn and repetition that he'd never understood, the spiral has thinned now and falters in this moment of perception. And he knows too, he's too scared to look out, just like he's too scared to turn.

The bitch sets up a yowling. From its tone and urgency, it can only mean that Denise is coming down the driveway. He moves to the window and, yes, it's her. She's not due home for hours, but he looks at her face as she opens the house gate and recognises a set to her jaw that will soon be discharging home truths in his ear.

He wipes away another of the persistent tears and is surprised to find himself sobbing into its wetness. It's no whirlwind he's lived in. This house at least, something built, together. If he's been locked inside his own agenda, there's always been someone next to him, spinning out her own progress with a wavelength so close he'd come to take it for granted. For decades they'd unravelled the same moment, holding the present together. If he can't see out, he can still see her. Past or present, she's there.

You come into this world out of love, sure, and maybe, if there's any left at the end, it's best to hand it on.

He steps out into the glare of the veranda to greet her and she looks up from the jollying she's giving the dog as it rolls around her feet. As her face rises, he sees it start to harden, then melt as his arms enfold her.

Raven

He's seen out thirty summers, but none as good as this. A hot nor-wester plays upon his ruff and he's proud of how it riffles, dancing from foot to foot, contemplating his next move.

Raven and Jet share the island of a dead cow's back. Slumped in mud, the last of the water, oily black, surrounds its final throe. The birds look down upon some fish that sluice this tepid shelter. Patiently the pair must wait.

The sun's heat grows. Jet stops her dance to stare at him. She leans across and sees a shred of flesh still clinging to his beak. They clash their bills together: a hollow rhythm, staccato grace, until the meat is left upon her beak. She slips it on her tongue. Raven's pride overflows and he calls on the sun to be his witness, his voice shimmering through the heat, higher than the dead tree summits.

Slowly, the fishes die so that Jet and Raven may jump down upon them. It is many years since Raven became aware of the fish, having seen them in a dream. Taking then a post above the dam, he saw that they were real. Where shafts of light betrayed the depth in which they moved, he pondered on their lack of wings. Raven's knowledge is of depth: the columns of air that none may see, he knows, likewise the cool currents of the heights. In that earlier time, he had looked down at the fish and was glad. He looks down now and grips one underfoot, watching himself fade from the mirror of its eye.

Other animals he understands less, it being an ungainly place, the ground. Raven has long seen the sick and old stumble and followed them down, always down. They might collapse against some fence, or in a bramble, but always at the lowest point that they could reach. There is little pity in Raven for those who are not his kin. Yet the stumblings of the land animals let him understand; unknowing, their feet are locked upon a ground that will one day pull them down. He does not pity or despise, he understands and waits. Shimmering, he abides, his ruff all iridescent. Jet looks across the silver rim of his eye, down into the depth beyond that edge. She croons there a song so low that only he can hear, the song of her love. He is her third mate, the others long dead and mourned. Now, they owe each other everything.

Across a threadbare paddock, magpies march in piebald rank. They watch each other forage, jealous of success, angry birds that Raven would not disturb lest their jealousy turn on him and ignite. Hidden in a tree, he switches his gaze to an eagle on the ground. Dull-gold feathers on the large bird's back break their sheen to tilt and part as she stoops to tear at a kangaroo's carcass; her beak scythes hide that Raven's bill could never cut.

It was not the habit of the farmer to kill the kangaroos, but this drought-summer has changed the man: agitated, he leaves his house day and night to lay waste to the grey animals, letting the bodies lie where they fall. The pickings have been good for eagle and raven, but taper now as summer extends and the farmer kills the last of the kangaroos.

Jet calls in the distance and Raven must respond. There is no particular urgency in her voice, so he keeps to the shelter of the casuarinas, following them up the gully and away from the magpies, gaining the heights of the ridge at the cattle yards by flying up a fold in the hill. Panting from the effort of ascent, he relaxes into a slow glide down the broad line of the ridge, towards his mate.

She waits on the edge of the steep bush block, peering down: forty tree-filled acres carved into the flank of their grassy ridge. Rough-barked apple gums shoulder each other, stunted, all ten metres high with dull grey leaves. Here and there, stringybarks emerge as tall green cones and beyond the bottom of the hill, through a shallow chasm, the river can be glimpsed.

There, the territory of other ravens begins and it is through this gap that intruders have come. Jet reaches forward to preen a greeting that Raven does not acknowledge. She was right to call but wrong to think it isn't urgent: the pair of young ravens scouring old blackberries along the bottom of the ravine include their daughter, two years old, who left last winter.

She left by choice to find a mate but now comes sneaking back, a stranger. The cock that accompanies her is the offspring of an alien pair. This poor ravine will not support the new mates and they will try to take more land. Jet and Raven are old and have not raised a chick since this hen. Without juveniles to support them, they have no choice and must drive the young pair away.

Jet was hatched high in the once living branches of the ring-barked tree in which she sits and has never known another range. She regards the return of her daughter complacently. Raven does not share the same response. He arrived here as a refugee, hunted out of every territory along the river. It is many years since he slipped unseen through the gate of this ravine to hide like these two birds. He knows the desperation that drives them.

Snubbed by his lack of a greeting, Jet looks at Raven and sees the aggression in his gaze. She takes its measure and tightens her plumage against a sense of dread that comes creeping from below. Suddenly, she sees the precipice on which they sit. She cannot stop Raven; he will attack.

Implacable, having height to dive and gain momentum, there is no other time than now to overwhelm the birds below. Without another glance, he launches from his perch, Jet sees him fold his wings as his dive begins to rocket. She had wanted to warn the youngsters off with a challenge but now stays mute, diving in pursuit of Raven. There will be no warning, no second chance.

The cock is reaching through a vine to wrangle at a berry, and then hears Raven's swoop. Slowed by thorns to disengage, he has no time to move before a brutal blow. Raven's beak cuts his back as the old bird's weight drives him down among the vines, tangling his wings. He thrashes and swings but Raven takes a grip, punching at the young bird's belly, turning the small hook on his beak, trying for a cut that he can drive hard into.

The cock cannot free his head or wings and as he struggles a thorn is scraped across one eye. He squawks in terror to his mate. The hen stands, mesmerised by the surprise and brutality of her father's attack. After an instant, she rushes towards the tangled males, but too late: Jet plants two feet into her back and drives her to the ground, aiming a peck at the young hen's nape. But, where Jet is old and uncertain, the hen is agile and animated by a sudden rage. She pulls to one side so Jet's blow misses, then strikes the parent with the shoulder of her wing. Jet's momentum has carried her off balance and the hen's blow sends her rolling on her back.

The hen is up and onto her in an instant, aiming for her eyes. Raven sees the tumbling pair and Jet upon her back, beak agape in stress and fear as she writhes to dodge the blows. He leaves the cock and rushes to her aid. The hen leaps aside and pecks as he approaches, then spreads her wings to pen him as she leaps to pin him down. He wedges in with lowered head then thrusts himself up high, sending hen a-tumble down his back. In between Jet and hen, he swings to face the challenge.

The cock, meanwhile, is thrashing clear of thorn and briar then flies away in panic. Hen has held her father's eye to show her lack of fear, but hears the beat of fleeing wings and leaps into the air. The pair, heavy in their rising flight, dodge trunk and branch while gaining height until they clear the trees.

Raven reaches down and nudges Jet to help her to her feet. She rolls instead and lies upon her belly with open beak and downward gaze. He smoothes the plumes along her head then leaps into pursuit, down the washed-out gully, straight and fast, gaining speed to clear the trees at a meadow that he knows. He follows hard behind the pair. Through the gulch, then racing down the river, swerving through the river oaks and banking through high branches.

Heedless of the brush of leaves, Raven gains on cock till he's clacking at his tail. Hen swerves high and drops back down to snatch at Raven's wing. He dips his back towards her and rams her to one side. She brakes hard with wide-swept wings and slews a hoary branch, then levels out and lines up straight, chasing dodging males, wings faster than her heart.

Down towards the granite gorge they pass above cleared fields. A peregrine bursts through their chase just to show them up as they climb above the river. Hen has closed the gap and heckles at her father, cock gasping for breath as Raven tears his feathers. Then he sees a raven group whose range they have trespassed. Old and young, they're swooping in so he pulls up high and fast. Hen turns around towards him, thinking that he's tiring, but feels instead the swoop and peck of several juveniles.

The older, breeding pair are hassling at her mate, so she sweeps on back towards him, both desperate to escape. Raven climbs up well away, back towards his home, looking for a thermal to ease his transit high above the cares and scrapes of other jealous birds. Once up, he sees his ridge, its grass and dotted trees. He wings his weary way across, though his cry is harsh and proud as he calls out for his mate.

There is no answer. Jet is gone from the bush block. Eagle has abandoned the kangaroo's corpse but nor is Jet there. He climbs back up to the cattle yards and perches on a rail, calling into silence.

At last he flies to the highest point, where a granite tor sits proud upon the hill. He finds her there in an adjacent tree, beside their old, untidy nest. She does not move when he lands beside her, nor extend her neck when he tries to preen. Raven looks around; it is not this land he cares about. He leans his head upon her back and leaves it for the moment, then croons in deep, vibrating phrases.

Drought renews the summer's strength beyond its turn of season. The farmer trucks in water and pays for hay to feed his bony cattle, ranging out in the night-time hours to kill competing grazers. There is no grass left, no beige of summer pasture: bare earth baked all day beneath a rampant sun breathes its heat at night upon the angry hunter. Down along the gully bed, the apple gums have shed those leaves the beetles didn't eat. Stark, their branches twist to supplicate the sun.

Hidden amid bars of shade and convoluted branches, two black birds watch the farmer with his cattle. He drives his truck among the mob, cutting bales of hay, casting them behind. Cowhide gaunt on top of bone, they bellow for the feed, falling out behind the truck in a thin, contentious line. Once a herd of diverse colour, now all as grey as dust. Kicked up by their hooves and carried on the wind, fine dirt swirls in turning gusts, drifting up to a jaundiced sky in mockery of clouds. The farmer stands behind his empty truck, looking at the herd. He lifts a hand up to his head, which he slowly bows.

Both birds see a bond between the farmer and these mammals. Unlike other beasts, they stay in places that the farmer has enclosed. Where kangaroos would jump a fence, they abide. Wombats push beneath the wire but cows will not extend the gap. The birds have seen how the farmer nurtures cattle but kills off other animals. To Raven, cows are common on the ground but strangers to the land and, like their farmer, best avoided.

Early in the summer when the dams were drying out, some cows were caught in mud and the birds had had a major feast, following the eagle who'd opened up the meat. Then, they found their eagle dead and strung up on a fence. Jet had sat beside the raptor and lifted up a feather. Dropping it, she raised her head and sang a mournful song, one that Raven had not heard in many years, though he knows whom she is calling for, and her anger and her fears.

Now, careful of his camouflage, he stays behind a branch to contemplate the man. But Jet stands bold upon their perch staring at the killer. He calls her softly but she will not turn.

Long ago, when Raven arrived as a young bird, another farmer had controlled these fields. Old and bent, that long-gone man had worked hard, building fences, ringbarking trees. He had struggled in the bush ravine, felling, grubbing in the earth at stumps he couldn't shift, until the ground itself began to slump, down towards the river. That old man had just dug harder, as if the ground and trees would change according to his wishes, until he met a sudden end in the middle of his toil, clutching at his chest, going down upon the ground the same as other animals.

Raven had seen it. He had seen and heard everything in his days of hiding in the bush block: the bang and kick of a farmer's gun, the plummet of another raven, chest first into the ground. How strange to see such useless wings trailing out behind. It was that farmer who killed Jet's last love. He who strung her mate upon a fence, like this man hung up eagle.

Raven leaves his cover to go and sit beside her, flipping his wings, crouching, reaching up to sift the feathers of her ruff. She lofts the breeze, crossing just above, landing light beyond his reach, staring now towards the cattle: the older cows are all in calf and due at any day. Skeletons that stamp and snuff, they butt the ground as they seize the hay. Ponderous of belly, more bloated than heavy, their paunches hang from jutting hips while ridge-back spines and ribs project as unconvincing cages. Particular ones among them look even less healthy than the others, and if this appears to interest Jet, it makes Raven worry.

A willy wagtail has found their perch and skitches round their heads. It flits around erratically, directly in their way, though Raven sees it distracting Jet in the middle of her brooding. Last week, a locust plague had swarmed these fields, and there are still a lot of hoppers over by the blackberry clumps. With this little bird as a welcome prompt, Raven grabs the moment, calling out for Jet to follow as he leaps into the air, heading for the locusts. The wagtail chitters as he chases Raven, then sees that Jet has loitered, still staring at the cattle. He dances back and flitters in her face, so at last she turns and watches Raven's flight, then topples forward off the branch, swooping, losing height to gain the speed she needs to catch up with her mate.

Their line of flight crosses the wasted tussock of the swamp and the clay-pan floor between the clumps is tessellate with cracks. Jet closes in on Raven. He sees her follow and slows his pace until they cruise with easy beats, side by side. Nor-west gusts and willy-willies have died away and a gentle breeze comes swinging from the east. It helps the birds as they progress up a broad ridge side, towards the crest of the bush block.

The ground, stripped bare of grass, provides little cover for insect or reptile but the pair see none despite a constant watch. A lone echidna trundles, too slow to raise the dust, marching fixed and straight towards the orange obelisk of an anthill. Raven looks at Jet, sees the fast, light beat of her wings and calls out his happiness with a slow wail. Her head nods with each wing stroke as she glances back and adds a harmony to his song. One thermal, circling up from a baking fold of the ridge, lofts them high above their range. They see the river far below, its channels braided with sand, and the blue-grey foliage of the sentinel oaks, still shady as their roots reach deep to drink.

The blackberry vines are now below and they circle down with wings swept wide. Long flight quills splay stiff and tight with downy feathers dancing light atop each wing. Near the ground they bank and round, curving to a clearing in the vines. There, they stall their swoop and land, each upon a weightless step. Locusts rise in panic with yellow wings that flip and flick, a medley, all around.

The birds are quick as they run and jive, leaping onto wing to seize the hoppers from mid-flight, with landings brief to dash their prey, leaving insect wings and legs behind them on the ground.

Thus engaged, they do not see the lace monitor. Longer than a man, he hides amid dry bracken that tangles through the briar. Lying very still, he watches with intent. He wants to taste the scent of the birds, but holds the flicker of his tongue lest they see the movement. The lizard knows hunger, nothing else, and the heat of the day has charged his muscles full of ready speed. A straight-line sprinter, the locusts were hard enough to catch. But now, if he holds his peace, the crazy flight of insects will surely bring a bird close enough to rush. He pulls his head slowly into dappled shade where no prey will see the glimmer of his eye.

Jet has landed in a dance, one wing out wide to counterweigh the foot she reaches high, seizing a hopper that has broken free of the long back legs she holds within her beak. Jet has forty years. She has seen goannas climb up trees to take her eggs and not been able to stop them. In turn, she has heard the baby monitors digging free of termite nests in which they incubate. Waiting patient atop the mound, she snapped the babies up. This lace monitor, rushing from its hiding place, is no surprise to her. Though wrong-footed, she sweeps her wings and clears the ground before its jaws can close. Flapping high to a handy branch, she looks back down upon the lizard and calls out her derision. That is when she sees the calf.

Seventy metres along the ridge crest there is a hole beneath the fence.

The body of the calf is on the bush block side, its head and a foreleg project through the hole, back into the open paddock. The first calf to drop, it was born this morning, healthy and on its feet within the hour. Stumbling under its mother's licks and testing out its gambol, it had tripped upon a wombat rut and sprawled beneath the fence. With its mother calling to it, it tried to scramble back, pushing one foot and then its head through the rusted, dangling wires, then torquing tight a trap as it swung its body round. Exhausted now in the afternoon, abandoned by its mother, it lies still as the sun.

Raven flies and lands by Jet and feels a certain dread. She launches down towards the calf and so he follows. Ants are there already, on the rims around its eyes. A trail of them are busy, to and from its anus. Its tongue is out and blue, but it looks up to the birds and blinks incomprehension. Jet shifts from foot to foot, looking back, sharp and brief, not burdened by uncertainty. Raven glances around, cautious of the mother's rush. From their high ground he sees her, way down along the paddock. Marching back, having had her hay, she is bawling for her calf. With her udder down and swinging tight, her need is obvious. Raven looks on past her and sees the farmer standing. He watches her with a hand above his eyes, then tilts his head above her march and looks up towards their ridge. Raven feels the sense of dread stab within his breast.

That night, beside the tor, he has a dream of Jet. Her mate of old and she are once again together. He sees them in the water, swimming with the fish. The water turns to river and flows on down the valley and through the granite gorge. On it flows, between a gap in the mountains where he himself was born. He wakes up to a different day. A mist is lying on the riverbed and the wind, now fully from the east, lifts freshly at his feathers.

Jet and Raven fly for their evening drink. There is one rock pool left along the river. Contested day and night by companies of birds that fight for its possession, this pool is not a place the ageing birds will visit. They fly instead to the farmer's concrete trough, where their weakness as an unsupported couple will not be obvious. But, open to the paddock and lacking the shelter of shrubs or boulders, it is a place they have to visit quickly. The only cover is the rusting hulk of the old farmer's truck that they keep away from.

The easterly breeze has stayed throughout the day, putting an end to the summer's heat. To the south, above the mountains where Raven was born, the heads of cumulus clouds are beginning to appear, their summits rolling over, glowing through the evening light. The air carries a burden that feels like extra weight on Raven's wings. Heavy on his mind is the memory of his dream and throughout the day he has kept a careful eye on Jet, following her, staying above, watching side to side. They went back to the calf this morning, but it was gone. This afternoon they have scouted a north-facing scree on the far side of the bush block, shifting stones where skinks are apt to lay late eggs.

Their approach to the water is the same as usual. There is no sign of the farmer, no frisking of his dog. They land and Jet bends straight to drink from the brimming trough. Raven marches along the rim, looking at the truck. One old door is wide ajar: it was not like that before. It's then he sees the farmer, moving fast. Standing smoothly from his stoop within the truck, he swings a gun above its roof and crouches to the stock. Raven looks at Jet and she isn't looking out. He leaps upon his wing as the farmer lines her up. And Raven swoops the gunner's sights, cawing harsh for Jet to fly as if alone he might defy the farmer.

She hears a blast and drops from the far side of the trough, swerving away in a flight that hugs the ground. Another blast kicks up dirt all around and one flight feather falls away, clipped from her wing by an unseen power. She looks from side to side for Raven, then risks a landing in the skeleton of a tree two hundred metres from the trough.

She sees Raven, on the ground, just in front of the truck. His wings are still working, turning him over and over in one spot, as if he tries and fails to swim. The farmer walks across, puts one heel on Raven's head and grinds it into the dust.

Night wells out of evening shadows that pool blue along the river. Through this darkness, Jet returns. Crouching beside her mate, she leans her head upon his back, eyes open, seeing nothing. The sky hangs with stars that shift and wink through currents of heavy air. In the south, the cloud march has cleared the dark line of the range and their churning summits flash and incandesce, at first in silence, then with distant thunder. The sound grows loud as the clouds consume the stars and Jet remains, unmoving.

The first drops are heavy and make her body shudder. She feels their chill and nestles close to Raven. He holds no heat but she sees no point in leaving. The blackness breaks with bolts of light that starken her despair and raindrops kick up dust that spits back down as mud.

Hours pass and the rain deepens, beating on the ground, pooling, streaming into channels that flow around the birds.

Wings splayed flat, lifted by the water, Raven starts to swing around her. She grips a wing to hold him back, but he begins to pull away. The current grows and she takes one step and then another, down towards the gully bed. He bumps against the concrete trough where the water starts to buffet. Jet loses grip, a lightning stroke shows him edging round the trough, she gives pursuit with flash-blind eyes to find him in a tussock and holds him with both feet. Rain falls down through thunder crack to sheet more torrents free.

They are carried on to the gully bed, where streams converge, and they are swept down towards the swamp. The water slows but still bears them on and Jet holds tight to Raven as they spin through bursts of light. She watches for his silver eyes as a mirror to the past, but the mash of feathers at his head has sunk below the water, as if he looks to somewhere else and has no eyes for her.

At the far end of the swamp, a netting fence is in the water, sifting shreds of grass and dung and straining threads of blackberry vine. This mass has formed a porous dam that banks a wall of water. In time, the water's weight exerts a force that breaks the fence, surging free to rush towards the river.

Their gully breasts a final, steep descent. The surge of water narrows here, lining up behind a spout that leaps between two boulders, then falling down beyond all sight amid a pile of granite tors. From down below, a voice booms back, deep from hidden spaces.

Morning sheens the surface flow. In the darkness underneath, Raven's broken body has found a fluid grace. Jet holds deep with one foot as sunlight slants upon her, sifting rain through points of light that die back into drizzle. There comes the portal rush, granite tors that lean together, dark current tumbles through and Raven is a thing of water that sluices through the gap. The deep voice names him with a change of note but Jet has lost her grip, plunging back with sodden wings upon a circling raft of dross. Exhausted, striking out, she gets a grip upon some briar that clings onto a rock. Her strength all ebbed, she levers up and lies atop the stone. The voice booms on but has lost its word for Raven, she lifts her head to look around and finds there is no solace. Her streaming feathers hold a weight that makes her lower back, lying flat upon the boulder as if she too were stone.

So cold, her mind so numb, time passes into daze. Drizzle declines and the sun breaks through again. The climbing orb that dries her feathers binds her to the rock with shreds of grass and other rot that infiltrate her plumage. All the while, the land and sky resound with cries from creatures creeping forth to find their world transformed by water. Jet just lies and waits: some bird or cat must surely come and rid her of her life.

It is the hen who comes, flying from the river. The young bird sees the water, roiling at its banks, and breaks forth from her hiding place, brimmed with confidence in the changing of the world: all is altered by the night and, surely, she and cock have now the right to confront and end the past. She sweeps up high into the freshened air to boldly state her challenge, and looking down sees the form of Jet, inert upon a rock. With wings swept back, she falls through sweep and curve, landing light upon the stone that holds the old bird fast.

Jet feels her daughter's shadow. She opens her eyes and the silver eyes that greet her own could just as well be Raven's. She tries to roll and stand but the strands that bind her give small shift. Her strength fails and she sags. Hen moves fast with head aslant to prop her mother's back. Then, reaching down, hen picks off shreds of grass.

Returning

The contract was for two months and he's glad of the money, and gladder still to be heading home. The old place. New windows should look great, colonial, metal fly-screens tight as a drum. He pictures the clean-glass view across the orchard but a vibration comes through the steering wheel to interrupt. A flat tyre, he realises, as the handling goes heavy. Too bad, the council's just graded off the corrugations so the road's been a dream run for once. Still, what's ten minutes? There's a big old yellowbox ahead, so he pulls in under its shade. No use cursing. He cranks up the music, reaching under the passenger seat for his pigskin gloves. As he steps out of the cab, a breeze stirs cool air through the perfect summer day.

A scream startles him, drawing his gaze high to the woody writhe of a tree branch overhead. One black eye peeks down from underneath a sulphur-crest. He steps back to return the courtesy and the cockatoo is flattered, strutting its branch, snatching a preen, working through a series of poses that emphasise the semaphore of feathers on its head. He watches the act. Same bastards wrecked the old window frames. Cedar. Tore big chunks out. For what? Fun? He looks around for a rock and finding none turns his back on the bird, reaching in to the dash to pop the bonnet. Ignored, the creature huffs its chest, tucks in where its chin would be and tilts its head to twenty degrees. The music on the radio turns to rap. The sulphur-crest swings up and vibrates.

Five minutes later and he's hefting the flat tyre onto its bracket. He slams the bonnet down and tugs at the fingers of his gloves. There's a whooshing noise on high as a squadron of white cockatoos come sailing down off Wheelbarrow Ridge. Orderly in formation, he hears a civil chirrup of avian dialogue pass between them. The formation flickers as it passes: three beats of the wing and then a glide, each bird at its own pace.

Corellas. He glances at the branch and the sulphur-crest is still there, watching the corellas too. 'You could take a leaf out of their book,' he says. The cockatoo screeches and flies away, yawing and swerving through the air.

He's home by lunchtime. The letterbox is stuffed to overflowing so he throws the lot on the passenger floor to be sorted out later, bumps across the tussock flat to the cypress hedge that hides the old house and pulls up at the gate. He takes the groceries in first, then lifts his valise and dumps it on the veranda. The day has warmed and he looks through the heat a minute as cicada song beats down off the timbered ridge. Floury bakers. There's just the power to do so he heads around to the shed, checks the batteries, water level, voltage, plugs in the inverter. Good to go, he heads inside to boot up the computer and check his emails. What's happening with the new windows? He'd hoped they'd be here already.

The bloody computer's in a bad mood but eventually convinces him that it really has no news. Well, I guess that's good news in itself, he thinks to ease his disappointment. He really had been hoping to get stuck straight into the windows. Oh well, he sends an email to the supplier asking for a new estimated date of delivery then steps back out onto the veranda.

He does like to keep himself busy. Thinks, could do with a drink, but catches himself and walks off quickly around the house to check on the best way to get the old frames out. But the sight of them depresses him, ripped and gouged by the cockatoos. Two months he's spent working underground. Bloody birds. At least the mine had been alcohol-free, so there'd been no temptation. Bugger it, he thinks, I'll go and give the fruit trees a drink.

It's a short stroll to the orchard and the trees look great, the mildness of the spring having grown into a well-watered summer. Though the fruit's coming in early, three weeks to New Year and he can see apricots already falling. Or what's left of them: the closer he gets to the tree, the more damage he sees, leaves stripped, over-ripe fruit scattered or shredded, whole branches hanging, partially torn off. It's like the thing's been hit by a hailstorm, although that can't be; all the rest are okay, plums, the peaches, unripe fruit like Christmas decorations. But the few remaining apricots all have bite marks. Seeing this, it dawns on him, it's those bloody birds again.

He purses his lips, puts his hands on his hips and circles the tree to assess the damage before he gets the pruning saw. Stumbling, he looks down and the body of another sulphur-crested cockatoo is lying extended in the rank grass. Oh, he thinks, feeling a moment of pity. He nudges the poor thing with the toe of his boot then jumps back as the bird reanimates, scything at his foot as it snaps its secateurs-like beak, then flapping pathetically amid an entanglement of paspalum.

He's not a vindictive man when sober. But these sulphur-crested cockatoos have given him considerable provocation. Though still, live and let live. But if there's one thing he can't abide, it's the sight of a drunk. And looking at this bird and smelling the ferment of over-ripe fruit, his fruit, amid the shredded fragments of which the bird still sprawls, he knows one when he sees one. He turns back to the house to get his welding gloves.

Armoured to the elbows with cowhide, he reaches down to grasp the sleeping bird. Supine, one wing is open and its head is tilted back, the beak gaping. It wakes and thrashes as he grabs it but he's got a firm grip. The screeching begins as he lifts it off the ground and it lashes its head around to bite. The man has second thoughts but can't let go. The strength of the creature is surprising, both in the manic tug of its feet and the uncontainable gyrations of its head. One wing beats his face and it hurts. For want of any further plan, he starts back towards the house and is surprised to find that the rhythm of his movement has a calmative effect. Ten metres and the bird is still; twenty and it has returned to its slumber. He tucks the gaping wing away and cradles the thing in his arms. It's almost like a baby, he decides, doing a circuit of the house to draw the moment out, jigging the small, recumbent figure in his arms.

Inside, he lowers it gently to the table and the bird's crest falls open, its eyes starting wide a moment later as if controlled by the yellow feathers. All hell breaks loose. He can barely contain the creature as it thrashes and flaps. The room resounds under a raucous gale of screeches and he watches the crest pumping up and down like a conductor of calamitous music. Each shriek shudders at the top end of its range as the crest becomes a strobe of sulphur. There are moments of paroxysm where the sulphur feathers spread wide and quiver, a Mohawk alignment, each quill curving forward. He sees then that the attachment of the first quill begins between the bird's eyes, colouring its sight, controlling its focus.

The man breaks into a sweat. A pair of scissors are lying on the table; he splays one hand over the bird's chest and sweeps them up with the other. It is hard to get a dexterous grip through the clumsy gloves but he manages. The blades of the scissors spread as they move towards the bird's head. Its beak swings to face the challenge but the man strikes first and two sulphur quills fall upon the table. Stunned, the bird stiffens, the remaining quills of its crest splayed wide. He strikes two more swift blows and they flutter to the table. The tone of the bird's shriek changes to a gurgle and the creature goes limp.

He gingerly releases his grip on the small body and it lies on the table as still as death, unseeing eyes half open. The man wipes his brow and wonders what he has done. Feeling a pang of guilt, he stands uncertain for a minute, watching the comatose bird, regretting the whole episode like the excrement on his gloves. Making a decision, he walks to the laundry to get a cardboard box and feels relief as he closes the lid on the bird. He puts the box in a dark corner. I'll check on it later, he tells himself.

Back in the orchard, he digs a hole two feet deep. He likes to dig, the physicality of it, and at the end there is always the hole to admire, clean-cut, a product of honest labour. Yes, he needs to keep himself busy. And there is nothing more therapeutic than digging, particularly when one feels anxious, or has a need to clear one's mind of troubling thoughts. He loses himself in the effort, weaving his personal mantra into the rhythm of his exertion. 'The power of now,' he mutters, 'all we have is the power of now.'

He pauses, reaching down to grasp a handful of soil, squeezing it. Released, it damply retains the shape which his fist has bestowed, but he throws it down, looking back towards the house as he rests against the long handle of the spade. All we have, the power of now. He drops the spade and, picking up the rake, begins the messy job of raking in the fallen apricots. The corrupted fruit is hard to gather, some sliding between the tines of the rake, others catching on the points, making the implement clumsy, then unusable. Cleaning out the clogged-up tines is a smelly and unpleasant task that he performs above the hole, letting the sticky fruit drop straight in. Soon enough, the hole is two-thirds full and there are no fallen apricots left upon the ground.

The excavated dirt has been retained in a neat mound which he lifts back to the hole, carefully, scoop by scoop, dropping it and trampling it until all is flush. He continues, scraping up excess soil to counter future subsidence, then disperses the leftover dirt into the surrounding grass. With one task complete, he replaces the spade with the pruning saw and cuts back the tree's damaged branches, gathering up the trimmings and carrying them to a pile of winter withies that he is yet to burn. Then, job well done, he looks around and there is no sign that anything has ever been out of order. Carrying his tools back to the shed, he locks them inside and turns to face the house. Reluctantly, he concludes that he has no excuse but to enter.

He once had many friends. The circumstances under which he'd walked away being a subject that he particularly avoids. It had been necessary, that's all he knew, if he was to be true to himself, his proper self. And in the absence of conflicting advice, he has come to believe that avoidance is his personal strength. Each moment empowers him, if he can just keep it straight.

He shuts the door behind him, picks up the fallen quills and puts them on the mantelshelf, then sits down to the table, looking uneasily at the cardboard box. When the lid starts to move, he feels the stirrings of unwelcome change.

The lid has two flaps. One lifts a little and drops, lifts again, wavers, then lowers again. The whole box then vibrates with a knocking and flapping noise and both halves of the lid fly completely back. A beak appears at the cardboard rim and seizes it, followed by the whole, tonsured cockatoo, clambering up to perch. The box tips sideways, throwing the streamlined creature to the floor, where it adds a barrel roll to its tumble, the momentum carrying it lightly to its feet.

It stands there for a moment like an acrobat expecting applause, looking at the man with one eye. He shows little response so the bird projects its chest, tilting its head forward with a dramatic flourish, one that passes directly into a state of confusion, as if this comic act has been subjected to some sudden, inexplicable outrage: one that is invisible to all but the bird. The man shifts uneasily in his seat. But the posture of the bird slumps. Its strangely altered head hangs low as it waddles to the man's feet. Instead of biting, it throws itself down and lies submissively with its head extended on the floor.

Five minutes pass and curiosity overcomes the man's caution. He reaches down diffidently and touches the bird. It remains inert. Emboldened, he slides his hands, little by little, beneath the creature. Still no movement. He lifts it up and lays it on his lap, where it nestles. Reaching out an index finger, he touches the bird's tonsure, soothing its pink skin. The bird responds by pushing its head gently against this stimulation, releasing a mild chirrup, not unlike the call of a corella.

'Hey, Kojak,' breathes the man spontaneously, navigating one gentle fingertip around the jagged stump of a quill.

'Hey,' replies the bird indistinctly, then more clearly, 'Kojak.'

The windows arrive later that day. The delivery guy seems rushed, appearing not to notice Kojak, seated now on the man's shoulder. The guy quickly derricks his load down from the truck and hands over the documentation with a grunt, looking anywhere except at man and bird.

Broad bands of midriff flab and a dimpled buttock are exposed during the guy's hasty ascent of his cab, but man and bird don't mind, both calling the same cheerful goodbye. The man fetches a trolley before the truck's dust has settled, wheeling the new windows around the side of the house. Man and bird look up at the old frames, neither seeing cause to mention their damaged state, and both are whistling from the top rung of a ladder as the first of the wind-moulds falls free.

Two days later and all the windows have been replaced.

'All we have,' begins the man as he wheels away the last old frame.

'Power of now, power of now,' shouts Kojak, riding expertly on his shoulder.

By the time of the summer solstice, the pair are inseparable. They converse across a wide range of subjects, although it is the habit of the man to both set the subject and correct the contributions of his friend. The bird seems happy enough with this arrangement, but increasingly distracted by chance sightings of other birds.

At night, the man ponders his good fortune. Kojak's unexpected companionship has made him happier than he can remember. During the day, he occasionally notices a regrowth of fluffy yellow tufts but quickly gets the scissors onto them. Surely, he ponders, it's not possible that Kojak would ever revert. He shares his concerns with the bird, but it just repeats them back as a stream of babble. Foolishness, the man thinks: normally when he asks a question, he knows exactly how the bird will respond. But now, when he is troubled by reasonable uncertainties, Kojak has nothing to offer. Will this bird let him down, as did the people of his past? He has overcome adversity in his life by the ruthless excision of negativity, from himself, through the exclusion of others. Surely, though, having saved this ignorant bird from itself, he can keep it on the straight and narrow.

As the summer progresses, Kojak becomes increasingly listless.

In mid-January a flock of corellas punctuate the green of a neighbour's lucerne crop with white commas. The man wonders if he should discharge a shotgun to disperse them but Kojak leaps from his shoulder, flying towards the birds, chirruping in imitation of their call. They lift from the ground and coalesce as a nebulous cloud that drifts or parts in avoidance of the darting Kojak. The cockatoo's call grows an edge and it returns dejected. That night it will not let the man clip its tonsure.

February, the man wakes to a splintering sound. He walks to the living room and sees a large sulphur-crested cockatoo outside the window, tearing chunks from the new frame. Kojak, like a reflection, watches through the glass. The strange bird observes the man and raises its crest towards him.

Kojak turns to follow the cue, hoisting some rudimentary quills, then swings back and neatly tears a splinter from one colonial crossbar. The man emits a shout and Kojak drops the splinter, flying in panic to the fly-screen door, hitting the mesh and falling to the floor. With the door now ajar, the bird climbs to its feet and pushes through, lifting into the air with heavy beats, and is gone.

He needs to steady himself. It takes an instant to decide that he is better off without that bird. Surely, it was always going to let him down. He realises, yes, he'd known it all along. No, they are all the same…

In the stillness, a cloud passes across the sun and the man blinks.

'I've moved on,' he blurts suddenly, one hand still anchored on the mantelshelf, adding 'with the power of now' as an unconvincing afterthought. His eyes refocus and he notices, next to his hand, the quills that he once cut free from Kojak's head. They lie as left, in disorder, each with its own particular curve and length. He'd never quite noticed that about these lemon-yellow clippings, of Kojak.

'He was all I had,' concludes the man in a whisper. Resisting a sudden urge to sort and realign the feathers, he goes outside to inspect the damage.

Sakura's Grip

The canopy is a dark sky, sifting sun into points of light that shift with every step. Her passage stirs the air beneath and slowly, the forest breathes around her. A sudden spray of humus strikes her leg and looking down she gasps. How big and close the lyrebird stands, indifferent at her feet. Sombre plumage, a shadow in the jungle, it spins to scratch the soil. Bird of gloom, she thinks, never having seen or heard of such a creature. Once again, it splays one foot and sweeps away a wave of litter.

Sakura's laughter animates the air, moving lightly through the trees. She crouches down to look.

Bird of gloom bows too, pecking at the moistness it has exposed. Sakura sees its tail sweep high and the underside is silver. And there is colour too, as of the forest tiger.

Sakura extends a small hand and the bird swings away its tail. It will not see her and does not flee. Sakura is grateful. She raises her phone and takes an image of the bird, bowing slightly, whispering, 'Thank you.'

And so Sakura sees her phone has lost reception. Though its clock shows time to call her anxious mother, waiting in Kyoto. Sakura promised before setting out that she would ring Mother daily. She will not break this obligation. Looking back along the forest path, she remembers the landslide. There, she had taken a photo and recalls having seen a bar of reception. She sets off, back along the track.

The path into the landslide seems different on return. This track was once a trolley-rail for a long-abandoned mine, but now it leaves its level course, winding upwards, dropping down, a wash-out in a gully. The footing of shale is intermixed with rubble and becomes irregular. Boulders grow in size as the path weaves between. Whereas the rainforest had allowed an extensive line of sight beneath its canopy, ranks of tea tree and cedar wattle guard the approach to the landslide, cutting off all view. The path traverses a slope that tilts and steepens.

Sakura emerges into sunshine and a sudden revelation of landscape makes her gasp again. Great cliffs surround her valley on three sides. They are painted walls awash with ochre and umber and stand two hundred metres tall. Green slopes break against their base as a tide of tree-clad ridges. Sakura is humbled by this containment of a valley in which she herself feels insignificant.

Though the landslide unnerves her, the sheer quantity of slumped earth and stone that buried the track and destroyed the forest are hard to conceive. More keenly, she observes that here the order of the marching cliffs is overthrown. Yes, a mighty face of rock still towers above the path, but differently: smooth and pale, it bears a wounded look, as if it has lost the certainty to withstand wind and rain. In places, there are corners and sheets of rock suspended on its face. Weighing many tons, they look set to fall and add their burden to the confusion in which she stands.

Still there is no reception. Sakura raises the phone, rotating herself. Nothing. She sees a hulking boulder, bigger than the home of her parents. Fifty metres away across a chaotic slope, it sits, bizarrely level in the shape of a cube. One face is red with lichen, the others cream or white. A ramp of shale and rubble allows access to its summit. The route across to its base is difficult, squeezing between boulders, clambering up, sliding down. But it is an adventure, though she will not speak of it to Mother.

Eventually she finds herself looking up at the cube and works her way below an overhang to reach the ramp. A honeycomb of eroded rock detaches beneath her hand, pouring sand and pebbles down her back, but she does not mind. At the top of the boulder, a bank of pale sand has been washed by rain around a seat-sized rock. Still there is no reception. No, one bar opens up only to drop out as she keys in Mother's number. Looking up from the device, Sakura sees that the ochre cliffs are hung with shadow, drapes of blue unfurling. She rises from her seat and looks towards the path.

After scrambling back through the overhang, she is uncertain about which of the many rocks she had earlier squeezed between. She makes a choice and wriggles through one gap, hoping it is the same way that she came. At the far side, she is still not sure but pushes on, crawling up a hummock and sliding down its other side. Nothing looks familiar now. She looks up to the sun, hoping to gauge the direction of the track but the sun is not where she expects and she clicks her tongue: how confusing the sky of this southern hemisphere. Taking another guess, she forges on.

For ten minutes, there are many decisions to be made about which way to squeeze, slide or climb. Sakura is beginning to feel tired and often finds the downhill choice preferable. Finally, a large gully opens across her path and its slopes are steep and loose. It is not safe to continue. Nor can she climb back up the rocky barriers that she has jumped or slid down.

She looks at the phone. It has two bars of reception. Calling Mother is out of the question, so she rings triple nine but gets no answer. Then, trying triple zero, she gets through. It is hard to make herself understood. The call-taker asks many questions about what address she is calling from, and patiently Sakura repeats that she is calling from the forest, lost. In time the call-taker compromises, asking for the name of the nearest town, which is very hard for Sakura to pronounce. Sakura giggles at her awkward pronunciation but the call-taker becomes stern and passes her to a supervisor. The supervisor allocates five unsuccessful minutes to obtaining the name of the nearest cross street, then settles for Wide View Lookout as an acceptable substitute. Finally the supervisor explains in a loud, slow voice that policemen and a helicopter will be dispatched without delay.

Sakura hangs up and looks to the sky. The sun is a delicate hand's width above the horizon. She looks back to her phone and its battery indicator is as narrow and orange as the bank of clouds that peek above the cliffs. She puts all thoughts of Mother from her mind. She thinks instead about her brother and how he used to tease her for being such a helpless girl. 'Why,' he used to say, 'you cannot even throw or catch a ball.'

There are many pebbles scattered around the edge of the chasm where Sakura stands, and in its base a large, clean rock is lying. By the time the helicopter comes and circles overhead, the clean rock is littered with small stones. The helicopter circles three times and she waves her anorak, but the machine flies away without giving any indication of whether it has located her.

Sakura's phone rings. A man named Brad explains in a heavy accent that the helicopter has in fact seen her and secured her GPS location.

'Yes,' Sakura breathes, waiting courteously to ask when it will return.

Brad continues, 'That helo's not winch-capable, mate, and the other's offline this arvo.'

She is still contemplating this sentence when he asks, 'Sakura, are you injured in any way or do you have any life-threatening medical conditions?'

'No,' she replies, certain this time of his meaning, intending to ask again if the helicopter will return before nightfall.

'Then, mate, yer gunna have to spend the night where you are,' he says. 'Stay exactly still. Do not move from your current location. We will come and get you in the morning. Do you understand?'

'Thank you,' replies Sakura, re-formulating her question. But the line goes dead.

She lowers her phone and sits, looking out across the forest, observing that darkness does not descend. Rather, the deepest colours of the day rise upwards, climbing cliffs like a tide that lingers in the sky. Night gathers in the valley floor and pursues the last of the sun, hushing the songs of birds and muting colour as it passes. Sakura hears one final, liquid voice and knows it is the bird of gloom: what other song could so dissolve in darkness? Silence follows, a buffer where different noises stir, small and distant in the gloom but growing harsh and drawing closer with the night.

There are shrieks, disconcerting from afar, but worsening with proximity. The body of each shriek vibrates around a gurgling, keckling wail. Worse, Sakura hears one shriek begin and travel through the air, ending in a woody thump, not very far away. Whatever these creatures are, they cannot be any type of bird. Sakura has read of giant bats and flying foxes and wonders if this might be some such creature. Then, she hears a swish of feathered wings, a large bird flying straight and fast. It intercepts one gliding, gurgling shriek and ends it with a strangling. The forest falls silent. Sakura edges back, feeling her skin crawl.

Hours pass and the noises gradually return. Sakura hugs herself against the chill and seeks distraction by listening to other sounds from more familiar creatures: the hum of a mosquito, how many types of frog are calling (three, no four), the more familiar twitter of small bat sonar.

Eventually, a swollen and lopsided moon appears above the rim of the pale cliff, sheening the vast screen of rock and bringing illumination to the valley. With this extra light, Sakura catches a glimpse of one gliding keckler, a creature as big as a platter but too square in shape to make sense in flight. Suddenly, she hears a thud among the rocks above. A tumble of pebbles is dislodged and rattles down around her. She stands, shivering, but not with cold. But the creature that drops onto the ledge is no bigger than a kitten. It has a busy, white-tipped tail and eyes that catch the moonlight as it snuffles. Sakura concludes that it is a kind of possum. Fear lifts from her heart and she steps forward, reaching down to touch the little animal. A large boulder gives way beneath her feet, tumbling out of its matrix under Sakura's weight, bounding into the precipitous gully, taking Sakura with it.

Dell has come to recognise her own anxiety. She used to think she was just plain angry. Stuck in this same old seat. All these years, ten thousand scenes gone wrong, broken people who look for blame, patients, co-workers, self. You tidy one up and another breaks down. These things that fragment, lives, cars, children, come raining, no, drifting down: as memories, unsifted, and lie upon my abyssal plain. Too deep, don't stir them up, she thinks, sitting still and staring straight ahead, suspended in a tempest, between the whirlwind and the engine.

The big machine yaws in a blur of rotors as Bendel works to keep its trim. Trees and shrubs hang in an untidy fringe over the edge of the escarpment and, looking left, Dell sees them passing in a rush. They thrash in the kerosene wake of the helicopter as if, just woken, they decide too late to shake a fist. To her right, the valley is a fastness, shifting its depth slowly through blue tinted air. Dell considers asking Bendel to move away from the escarpment edge. She feels queasy. He's only following the line of cliffs so he can play the machine along their updraft. He's like a big kid. But he's the pilot, he'll do what he wants. Hopefully he'll get bored with this. Or Bradmate will give us something to do. After circuiting the valley for an hour, the fuel gauge is dropping.

Sure enough, Bendel's disembodied voice pops up in her headset and he's tired of doing laps. He says he'll call Brad on the helo channel and ask for an update.

Bradmate says, 'Maate! The cops have finished flying grids and they're head'n' off for fuel. Here's yer chance. Get in low and spot her in the rocks. Dunno why she's wandered off. She'll be head'n' back up to the track. Find her. We need a good result!'

Dell rolls her eyes. It was obvious from the outset that this shouldn't be a helicopter response. It's ridiculous, she thinks, that they didn't get a ground crew down to the girl. Did they seriously think that a tourist with poor English skills and a demonstrated capacity for getting lost was going to be in the same place they left her overnight? Plus four and a half hours of lonely daylight, the same time it took to get this helicopter on line. Having worked an afternoon shift yesterday, Brad shouldn't even be on duty. But he's got his paws all over this job. She wonders where the politics lie: helicopter budgets, foreigners? She shrugs.

Her stomach knots as they bank right and slew into the valley. After a moment, the machine levels, then leans back, nose higher than tail in a powered glide to the base of the landslide cliff. She watches the approach of the cliff and an extra heartbeat thumps her chest as the clatter of the rotors reverberates.

She says to Bendel, 'Listen, Ben, I know Bradmate said we should scout the rockfall, but I think we'd do better to check out a gully or two, downhill from where she was last seen. Tired walkers never go uphill and I know there's a lot of lawyer vine down there. She's probably just tangled up and tired.'

Bendel is startled by her voice: he hasn't worked with sullen Dell before, but he's heard enough about her to take her advice seriously. He's surprised she remembers his name, she says so little. Surprised and a little flattered, despite her use of the diminutive.

In the ninety years since the landslide buried the rainforest, a mixed forest has regrown around its lower fringe. Uniform in height as well as age, the trees stand nearly forty metres tall. Dell drags her eyes away from the sheet-rock of the soaring cliff, past its apron of rubble, and looks at the canopy of the trees, studying the colour of the foliage. Fresh tips of red and yellow on the eucalypts, bright green of apple gum, the turpentines are all blue-grey. Dell sees the treetops begin to writhe under the downwash of the helicopter and the machine bucks a little as it settles into its own buoyancy. Bendel levels out his little ship and they set sail across the billows of a seething canopy. All eyes peer downwards. They cross a big gully where a finger of rubble follows a wash-out off the lower landslip.

Then, at an angle through the foliage, below an understorey of tree ferns, Kev the crewman sees an anorak being waved. 'Dunno what the fuss is all about,' he says. 'There she is.'

Bendel follows the crewie's finger and replies, 'Well, looks like its time for the winch.'

Dell groans. This is what she has been dreading. It's not that she's scared. What worries her is that she feels no fear at all.

She puts on the usual show and no one notices the confusion she feels, cinching her harness, detailing the drugs and dressings in her thigh pouch…morphine, metaclopramide, midaz, okay. It's a recent thing, this uncertainty. It's been getting worse. She has a growing sense that something will go wrong. After eighteen years, statistically, it's time. But the thing is, she doesn't care. Indeed, does she welcome the idea? Is she cracking up? She tries stowing these thoughts in the usual places and partially succeeds.

She clumps over to the door and Kev checks the fastenings on her harness before tethering her. That done and having double-checked his own anchors, he slides the door wide, leans out into the hurricane and releases 1.2 metres of slack off the drum, clips Dell in and releases her tether. 'Okay,' he says. 'Good to go.'

Dell unplugs from the intercom, lowers her visor and rotates, grabbing the door rail before swinging smoothly onto the skid. Kev takes up the residual slack and she leans onto the cable, looking down at the writhing foliage.

The crewie reaches out and raps hard on her helmet, once, twice, giving her the thumbs up and mouthing the words, 'It's a jungle out there,' as she looks up, startled.

It's a little ritual of his that she loathes: it catches her every time, just as she starts to concentrate. She has a sudden urge to punch his stupid, grinning face, but hates herself for it.

The descent is spectacular. The trees are huge, pachydermatous turpentines like armour-plated pillars, the white shafts of the blue gums are two metres across and rise as serene columns for twenty metres without a branch. But it is the smooth-barked apple gums that glow, orange visions having shed their bark. Like most angophoras, their branches are extensive, horizontal and elegantly convoluted.

In passing, she looks along the length of one massive limb, absorbing the sight of fleshy bark freshly dimpled, some dimples open and clean, others plugged with last year's smoke-grey rind. At the far end of the branch, next to the trunk, a powerful owl crouches, weathering the buffets of the downdraft. Dell sees the baleful look it gives her and bursts out laughing. That bird looks like she feels! Offended, it prepares to fly away.

At first, between the racket of the chopper and the earmuffs in her helmet, Dell has little opportunity to understand what has really offended the bird. Able to hear what Dell cannot, it can also feel its branch cracking under the weight of the downdraft. Then, when one taloned foot begins to feel the timber groan and sever, it knows the time has come to launch itself, something an owl is loath to do during daylight hours. Its other claw holds the empty hide of the yellow-bellied glider it caught the night before. Released, the square cape of the possum spins away, resuming an interrupted flight.

Bendel, with Kev's help, has done his best to hover on one side or other of the largest limbs, but the science is inexact. Dell is ten metres below the owl's branch by the time it fully detaches. A twist in the angophora's limb catches onto the winch cable and the entire branch follows this sliding anchor. Dell feels the movement and looks up in time to see the main body of the brittle limb snap at a hollow and fall clear. But a serpentine length of timber still grasps the line and comes railing down towards her.

Kev holds tight, watching keenly. He knows his job: a helicopter crash five years back reinforces his understanding of every working moment. He sees the impact of the branch on Dell and waits, not long, as the branch pivots. Feeling his platform tip and yaw, he concludes that she's entangled and pitches out one arm, engaging the wire cutter and leaning hard on the lever while he still has time. With the cable severed, a sudden loss of load confuses Bendel and the machine lifts vertically, spinning and skidding through the sky. Kev is pitched out the door, swinging from his tether, trying without luck to see what has become of Dell.

The sleeves of her anorak whip fiercely as Sakura watches, appalled. The helicopter person plummets, a cable lashing and glinting in her wake. Large pieces of log are falling too, striking the ground and rebounding with sprays of dirt. Sakura crouches low but sees the person strike into the crown of a tree fern, bursting its parasol of fronds, sending tender croziers flying. The trunk flexes momentarily and snaps, toppling over an entanglement of frond and human that have already struck the ground. The turbo scream of the helicopter retreats into a wounded syncopation, but Sakura does not hear.

She grabs the large stick she has been attempting to use as a crutch. The slope between her and the fallen person is steep. With one shoe off, her bent and swollen foot is awkward and catches amid the barbs of a widespread vine that hides amid the fern and grass of the slope. Sakura hops upwards, wincing, ripping free of spiny tendrils.

She lies amid a heap of fronds and scabby, hairy tree fern trunk. Sakura stands above her, finding it hard to tell a helmeted head from a pair of boots amid such wreckage. Then, as silence returns to the forest, Sakura hears the stridor of laboured breathing that leads her to a face: the visor cracked, mandible and jaw pale and embedded with splinters. Her upper lip is torn half off with missing teeth and damaged gums.

The chest shudders with each attempt to breathe. Sakura winces as she kneels, reaching an index finger into the person's mouth, clearing out mucus, fragments of tooth and wood, seeking to open the airway. But the stridor persists. The upturned face is turning blue. A jugular vein stands out, engorged above the helmet strap.

Sakura tries aligning the head but the stridor changes into a whistle, then stops. The helicopter person's body goes rigid, straightening to its full length and arching. This exposes a breast pocket from which a pair of clothing shears project. Sakura grabs them and cuts the helmet strap, pulling the casket clear as gently as she can. The body relaxes and the woman lies completely still. Then, slowly, quietly, her breathing resumes.

Sakura concentrates, uncertain what to do next. She decides to clear away some shrub and roll the person on her side. She must also cut free a bulging pouch located on the thigh, but uses it as a pillow for the woman's head. At last she sits and holds the woman's hand, waiting.

Dell comes up slowly, feeling like every fight she ever lost. From a depth, she ascends towards light that splits her head with pain. Becoming aware of her mouth, she probes her tongue into an unfamiliar aperture and blood flows down her throat. She coughs and each cough grips her chest like talons. Her eyes open onto dappled, blurry green and she tries to roll onto her back, but something stops her. The tree, the cable, she remembers! Lie still, she thinks dully. Check yourself over. Not anxious to explore her mouth again, she groans and moves her feet, and they move okay. Likewise, her one free arm can flex, but again something reaches out to hold it.

She remembers that there had been a patient and tilts her head, trying to focus. A hand moves across her line of vision to soothe her brow. Dell hears gentle words spoken, but cannot understand them. Swivelling her head, she looks up and a face comes into focus, peering down upon her.

The patient, I have to check the patient, thinks Dell. But, she realises, it is the patient who holds her still. One hand grips her own, squeezing it.

Dell tries to speak but cannot make a sensible noise. Another trickle of blood triggers more stabbing coughs. When she looks up again, the patient's face is very sad. Tears are streaming down it. The sight has an unexpected effect on Dell, turning her coughs into sobs. The sobs rise painlessly from the depth she left behind and she surrenders to them. Her tears release, and the more she sobs the more she feels Sakura's grip.

Stepping Out

Alan Dougherty slips from the side door. They wont miss him, and he certainly will not miss them. They'd taken away his chair, that was the final straw, hot-desking! Damn their eyes. Truth is, though, he hadn't had the courage to confront Glenda. She was the one who was behind it all. He stands on the footpath wondering how long it'll be before they notice him gone.

Someone bumps into him, slopping half their coffee over his shirt and trousers. They curse, not so much at Alan Dougherty, as through him, as if he were a lamp post that had crept into their path. And a lamp post is only okay if it knows its place. Alan starts reaching for his handkerchief to try and clean himself up, but stops.

He spins around to tell that clown to keep a lid on it in future, cup, mouth, whatever! But the coffee drinker is gone, just people rushing by, indifferent even to the imprecation of his raised finger. Mustn't stand here, he thinks, lowering the finger, hiding it amid a pudgy fist that, embarrassed, he looks away from as he lowers.

From the side door you can go uphill onto Market, or downhill to Darling Harbour. Alan Dougherty takes the downhill option. But he surprises himself by turning right into Sussex. It's eleven-thirty. How could he possibly go home? What would Cheryl think?

He finds himself alone below the Western Distributor. The sound of traffic rebounding off glass and concrete does not permit much thought, but he pauses in the sea of white noise. He still sees Glenda's face. She had actually sneered: the quality of management at Baker and Sloane had been in decline for years. Although, he thinks, the more their slogans about the Team and Best Practice, the less polite they'd grown. As quiet words of encouragement had become unheard, so too the fortunes of the company had declined, until the parlous threshold of insolvency came looming and, with it, Glenda.

She'd come over from the health sector, it was said. The ill-health sector, thought Alan: wizened, she'd looked like a little old Egyptian mummy, unwrapped, reanimated by dark forces to do the dirty work. And her nose was always runny. She had a particular way of talking that emphasised the natural prominence of her teeth. It was quite unnerving. It was she who had replaced slogan with outright threat.

A Harley Davidson blats and bellows overhead. Alan moves on.

At the underpass to Hickson Road, a homeless man occupies the footpath. Alan Dougherty becomes uneasy. He doesn't like the stare of vagrants, how they always seem to lift their gaze and bathe him in their private world. This lack of social boundary is something that he finds, well, too inclusive. And now this fellow's gaze, unfocused, seems yet able to filter out those jaundiced facts that Alan holds as private.

Through the traffic rush, Alan hears him thinking, 'Hey, mate, welcome, sit yerself down.' He turns away between some columns, through concrete aisles, a smell of piss and the drift of fumes from overhead. Perhaps I should go back, thinks Alan. But an alley opens on his left and he lets himself swerve in. A ceiling closes in, shopfront windows daubed with white that echo, all unlet. A breeze pursues and drifts him through to Kent Street with just his feet a-slap to mark the passage, and a bus pulls up that he finds himself inclined to board. But it shuts its doors with a flatulent hiss and rumbles off.

There is no hoarding above him now and he lifts his eyes to glass and concrete towers, an aperture of sky. Solitude. His breath lets go. With none to witness, calm descends and he finds the footpath is a kingdom where he opts again for north, towards the sun. He realises, yes, it would be his pleasure to see the harbour, laid out in spangles far below. No thoughts of Glenda now.

The Agar Steps are sandstone, a sepia progression that carries him on high. A rounded hill, a sward of grass, long-armed figs with buttressed roots, some with light bark, some with dark. He moves towards a rolling crest where his gaze soars out beside the bridge. Yes, the harbour. He sighs and settles down upon the grass, tries to collect his thoughts, reaches for his phone instead, then puts it down beside him. No! No need for messages: damn social media. But in a minute – yes, just a minute – he'll make that call to Cheryl. Ah, but now to see again the sea! A cruise ship crowds beneath the span, the soar of gulls, one small sail that changes tack and, flapping, falters for a moment.

A sudden blow to the back of Alan's head is no less startling for being light. He suffers a moment of dread as something grips his hair and flutters, swings around and a myna bird lets go, snapping at his face with yellow beak and piercing him with screams. He shields his eyes with one forearm and, rising to his feet, lashes with the other. The myna dances light on air, waiting for another chance to strike, then lofts away onto a branch and pipes for reinforcements. Alan looks around and sees more grey troops coming, marshalled worse by a magpie swoop, its red-eye scowl and a cowl of white a blur as it hurtles past and rounds. Alan makes a run for it.

He sees a bottle on the ground, reaches down to snatch it, then jags out right as he hears a swoop behind. The magpie rockets, Alan pivots as he runs, hurling bottle after hostile bird. He has always had poor aim and never for a second expects to connect, yet trajectories of glass and bird intersect and the magpie tumbles down. Alan stops, upset, walks across to the deathly bird and lowers to his knees. But it shuts its gaping beak and squawks, rolls upon its feet and staggers off. After ten metres, it quickens to a groggy run, becomes airborne and flies away, uneven.

With the humbling of this persecutor, Alan feels an exultation. He stands and turns to face the mob of mynas that mill and swoop as if to harry, but safely at a distance. Alan projects his chin at their shrieks, sniffs and turns away. A looping path of old macadam leads him down to Argyle Street, then onwards to the Quay.

He is not sure what he is doing here. He doesn't like being crowded. He steps around a human statue, dodges past a juggler: he could keep on walking to the Opera House, go on from there to the Gardens, but a big crowd is visible on the forecourt steps, and the Manly ferry is at its wharf, proud and tall, facing both ways on the water. Alan buys a ticket and is the last across the gangplank.

There are few aboard at this time of day but Alan sits outside. A hair-gelled boy observes his phone while spitting on the deck, one well-dressed lady shelters behind large sunglasses. Cheryl, Alan thinks, I must ring Cheryl. Can't just go sailing off to Manly. Must explain the facts. She will understand. He reaches for his phone and finds it missing, remembers, damn, the birds. How could I explain the facts anyway, he thinks. They're hopeless. I'm hopeless. The ferry rounds the Opera House, Alan bows his head, burying his face in his hands. The woman shifts her opaque gaze, just slightly, in his direction.

She waits until they pass by Pinchgut and Alan hasn't moved, takes off her specs and smoothes her hair, edges close to Alan. 'Are you all right?' she asks him kindly, touching his shoulder.

Alan looks up with red-lined eyes and the eyes that greet his are warm and kind. He feels embarrassed, lost for words, would turn away but does not wish to be impolite.

Through a strangely steady gaze she says, 'You just look as if you've had some bad news, that's all, as if you're a little bit lost.'

Alan considers both aspects of this pronouncement and reacts with sudden panic. 'Why, isn't this the Manly ferry?'

'Of course it is, silly,' she responds with an indulgent smile, her hand still on his shoulder. Then, more earnestly, 'Perhaps you just need someone to talk to, that's all. You know what they say about a problem shared?'

'Err…' replies Alan, trying hard to think.

'I've been unhappy too,' she swiftly continues. 'I know what it's like!'

Alan sits up straight and turns to face her: she is mature, about his age, but still a beautiful woman. And, he thinks, very neatly groomed. He feels flattered and worries that he might blush, a worry compounded by her unwavering gaze. He raises one hand subconsciously to shelter his face but intercepts it in time to adjust his tie, only to find he isn't wearing one. She drops her hand to her lap, where it clasps its twin, tilts her head until her hair drapes gold, and holds him in her smile.

An awkward silence weighs on Alan. It's my fault, he thinks, I should be debonair.

She unclasps the hand again and reaches out, placing it on his. 'It's okay,' she says. 'Just be in the moment. You can find yourself in silence, you know, below the noise.'

She looks around at the rumblings of the ferry for a second and, mystified, so does Alan. But when he looks back, none the wiser, he finds her waiting with her stare.

'Your true self,' she continues, leaning forward without a blink.

The moment extends. Alan feels like a small creature crouched against the back of its burrow. He wants to remove his hand, but still does not wish to offend, would look away if he could. He makes an effort and his vision escapes as far as her eyebrows, but they arch high and fixed like a smoothed-out frown, an effect that draws his focus inexorably back to her eyes. In the stillness, her hand is becoming clammy and Alan starts to sweat as well. Then a movement at the edge of vision helps him look away. It is the boy: he has lowered his phone and is staring at them, smirking. Once observed, he looks away with a sneer.

'Erm,' says Alan as he draws his hand clear, 'yes, er, thank you. Excuse me a moment.'

She tries to edge closer but he stands quickly and walks to the handrail. He keeps his back to her as he wonders if it would be appropriate to simply walk away. But the ferry now is passing the Sow and Pigs and Alan becomes distracted by the sight of a line of bubbles that have escaped the churn of the rocks. The trail of bubbles comes fizzing towards the ferry like a torpedo closing in. There is a silver flash in the depths below and he sees a shape flip back into something dark, racing underwater. Finally, a little penguin bobs to the surface beside the boat, holding a whiting in its beak. The fish flaps and writhes, but the penguin will not let go. Alan observes the bird, its brick-shaped body and stubby wings, wondering how such a small, ungainly creature could possibly survive at sea. There is a sudden yapping noise as a second penguin surfaces beside the first, which reaches out with its fish. The second penguin takes the whiting, head first, and quickly gulps it down. Both birds then clack their bills together, shaking their heads in a dance-like display, and disappear again below the surface.

Alan smiles as the ferry moves on, the vision of the two birds lingering warmly in his mind. It is a moment he would like to share, so he turns to face the lady. But, in a strange reversal of circumstance, she is now crouching forward with her face hidden in her hands.

Forgetting the birds, Alan worries that he may have hurt her feelings and sits back down beside her. 'Are you okay?' he asks.

She lifts her face from her hands and, still bent forwards, turns it towards Alan. The face is flushed now, the eyes wet. 'Seven thousand dollars,' she says through gritted teeth.

Alan purses his lips and pauses on the edge of speech, uncertain. He leans politely forward to return her gaze, his mouth working silently as he wonders if there is something that he has missed.

'The life coaching course I did,' she continues, 'it cost me seven thousand dollars.'

'Ah!' replies Alan, sitting up as if free of confusion.

'They said it was guaranteed, success or your money back,' she continues, watching him from the crouched position. 'Well, nobody's buying it. Least of all you.' She sits up, extending her legs in front of her, looking up towards Bobbin Head. 'And they won't reply to my emails, won't answer the phone... I've gone back to their office today to try and get a refund, but the whole place is empty. They're not even there any more!' She has begun to wave her arms, but stops and turns her face to Alan. 'Think I've got seven grand to throw away?'

Alan observes that the gold finish on her vinyl shoes is flaking and says, 'No.'

'Damn right,' she replies, turning away again, kicking loose the shoes. She has a painful-looking bunion on one foot.

They sit in silence, side by side.

'Bastards!' Alan adds after a while.

'Reckon,' she replies.

Alan considers sharing his observations about the penguins, wondering if it might help to cheer her up. He decides, no, but has a sudden thought. 'I don't mean to be rude,' he says, 'but there's someone I really need to ring. Would it be okay if I could borrow your phone?'

She pauses for a second as if considering a transaction. Then shakes her head and shrugs her shoulders, and with a sigh says, 'Sure.'

The Mixed Success of Suzie Dyer

The eyes of Justice Flegget are no less fierce for having shrunk, peering down atop thick lenses. His brow is creased and his lips are pursed, like sucking on a lemon. The mood of his court has soured.

Suzie Dyer shifts her seat, trying not to laugh. She snatches up a handkerchief and fakes a sneeze, expelling sobs that have gathered in her chest, then hides her face a moment longer to pat down her mascara. How cruel is memory, that agent of entropy which will not be suppressed. Again it hoists the image, ten years old, of Flegget in the gutter, disgraced again outside the Star Hotel. It had been a common, post-court occurrence when Flegget had been the barrister, when she was just his junior, the one on the bottom rung, the scapegoat for a brief gone wrong.

She spins her eyes clear of the pompous arch of his eyebrows, saves a tottering stack of folders as they start to topple, and lowers her gaze to Kate. The young solicitor crouches forward in the seat next to Suzie, beads of sweat pilling on her brow as she rats through one shabby file after another. A lone silverfish darts from a tired folder and swarms onto Kate, disappearing amid her sober pleats. Suzie feels the sobs regroup and jostle at her ribs. Her fight is lost; she leaves the folders to their fate and sobs into her hanky. For her mascara, there can be no hope.

Seated on her left, Senior Counsel Cassamerti is leaning forward to see past Suzie, glaring at Kate out of a headache. There is a bad taste in his mouth and he resents this interruption to a private train of thoughts: the apprehended violence order his wife has taken out may lack relevance to today's case, but is for him no less pressing. This shambles is Dyer's fault, he concludes; you can't trust any of them. He'll tear strips off these two later. Suzie turns to look at Cassamerti and her mirth dries up. She reassures him with a wry face, but it's an easy guess that he's behind the missing status of the amended statement that Kate is searching for. Granted, it could be some ploy of the witness, who is saying now that he scanned it to an email, but the facts remain that Cassamerti has lately lost the plot.

She looks across to the table of the opposition, expecting to see the hostile team in a similar state of flux, if not outright panic. But suited up as black as penguins, the trio are sitting cool: Sally inspects her nails, Selwyn nods to the judge's every rumble; the third one seems to be asleep. Suzie tilts her head: the missing paperwork is certainly an embarrassment for her own team, but if the altered statement does exist, and backs up what the witness claims, it will be a disaster for the other table. *Ipso facto*, they could only look so cool if they have a copy somewhere and have already planned their game. So the witness is telling the truth and Cassamerti has blown the paperwork again!

Suzie leans forward in her seat, shielding Kate from the auger of her senior counsel's stare. The witness, alone in his box, looks flustered and confused. She catches his eye and holds it, smiling at him the kind of smile that never fails to make men pause.

'Get an adjournment off Flegget and a copy of the amended statement off the witness,' she murmurs to Cassamerti. 'We'll cook their arses with this.' She releases the witness from her gaze and, pressing shut her smile, holds it warm inside.

Cassamerti stands as asked, discharging his bluster against the wall of Justice Flegget's bench. The old scoundrel peers back down with a pout, having heard it all before. At last he sighs and grudges them twenty minutes to copy and review the original of the amended statement that the witness claims to have in his possession.

Suzie gets to her feet and watches as the judge stands and limps off, musing on the path of a career that has led her to this chamber, this catacomb, the Coroner's Court. She puts away her hanky and shuffles out behind Cassamerti, determined to salvage some tactics from his swamp of woes.

She shuts their door and pours three coffees, handing one to Kate.

Kate trembles as she takes it. Cassamerti starts a tirade but Suzie stares him down. He blusters into silence.

She lets it stand for a moment, then says, 'We need to pin this witness down, get a double take on where his altered testimony is going to land. Because I think it's going to land right in our court.'

Cassamerti gets fired up, acting as if he is behind the new plan, insisting that he will go and confront the witness outside. Suzie feels a moment of regret: the witness is either naïve or desperate, trying to wing an agenda from the witness box, but she likes his nerve. The fact that Sally Winter is fronting the opposition team means that the Health Minister's office has a particular interest in this case. They don't often let her off the leash. They'll be cooking up a cover-up, or after a scapegoat, the witness most likely.

'We need to support the guy,' Suzie says to Cassamerti. 'His testimony is the egg we need to crack, gently,' she adds, wondering whether Cassamerti could tell a soufflé from a plate of scrambled eggs.

They all look up expectantly as the clerk bustles in with fresh photocopies of the amended statement. Cassamerti snatches a copy and heads straight out the door. But that's okay, thinks Suzie, he's the one who stands up before the judge. The witness will sink or swim of his own accord, but when the time comes, Cassamerti is going to be asking the right questions. She thanks the clerk, sits down and reads, gleaning fact after fact from the statement's every awkward phrase. Thirteen minutes left.

The brine hisses up the slope, fans out and dies into the sand. Footing along the waterline is firm and each fan has left a pattern that she passes over with pounding feet. Filigrees of spume lie trapped where the patterns interlink, never quite the same in their fish-scale overlap. One wave surprises her, surging up to douse her legs in passing, erasing the old as it swashes in the new. A sheen off the sun's first ray steeps colour on the strand and she calls out a greeting to the orb, her voice jolting as she runs. Further up the beach, a tractor is sifting the sand for shattered glass and needles. For fun, the driver homes in on a flaked-out backpacker and the young man wakes to the clatter of the machine. He staggers away, cursing. Suzie adjusts her music and begins the return lap.

The climb back up from Coogee Bay steepens as the sun's heat grows aggressive on her back and, around her, the city builds into the discord of its day. Bougainvillea hangs in striking masses upon retaining walls, hiding cracks in concrete and the fading paint of tags. She wonders as she runs, who was Bougainville anyway? Thinks of an old client, a worn-out bogan with bad teeth and florid skin. His stories had been cracked but had retained some elements of truth.

Crossing Avoca Street, a 373 blares its horn at her as it races through an amber light, but she does not stop until she reaches the Belmore Café, two blocks short of her unit. The lycra on her legs has dried and she pauses on the threshold to brush off clinging sand, thinking of Rick, wondering when he came here last. She straightens, sighs and walks straight in.

Brendan looks up from behind his coffee machine and is glad see her. Rick used to say that looking into Brendan's eyes was like looking into her own. She'd chided him for fancying young men while relishing the comparison.

The lad calls out, 'Hey, Suzie, the usual?' but she walks to the counter to confirm her order, to see the greenness of his eyes. He looks up from his labours and smiles patiently.

She turns away embarrassed, wondering how he sees her: as an old hen? Broody? How many middle-aged women clad in lycra would he encounter here every day? A clock is mounted on the wall, she looks away from its ticking, thinking again of Rick. Had she made the right choice?

As she sits, jaunty Selwyn Pike comes cruising along the pavement. His stride is smooth for a heavy man, and his jaw thrust out. He has hungry eyes. She ducks low in her seat, but too late. He swerves straight into the café. Stately when poised, he blocks out Brendan's sun, lifting his baritone to demand a complicated arrangement of decaffeinated coffee and milk substitute. Only then does he turn and feign surprise to see her.

She's been waiting for it and chimes in first, saying, 'Selwyn, that coffee's quite a wank. Sure you can afford it?' He needs to understand, she's not his small fish.

Pike ignores the jibe and sits down uninvited, replying, 'Not after the way your Cassamerti kicked Sally and me around the Coroner's Court, Suzie dear. Still, good to see the old coot on top of his game.' Adding, 'A smart lass like you can pick up a few pointers there!' He wants to sweeten her demeanour, which he has noticed is short. Selwyn Pike prides himself on his powers of observation.

Suzie's own tendencies include a predisposition to identify and antagonise conceit, predatory married men and persons of any sex who habitually broaden their options by believing their own spin. She notices the Riverview cygnet on Pike's right hand and cocks her head to prepare a suitably Jesuitical line of attack. Pike, waiting, sees a slight smile grow on her face and congratulates himself on his initial play.

It's only then that Suzie catches the movement at the door: Rick, peering around the shopfront, trying not to be seen. But even the light at his back cannot conceal the upset on his face. It's been three months since she took his last desperate phone call, two months since she changed her email address and two weeks to the day since she'd cleared away his final text. It had read, 'I don't mind if you really don't want kids, I just want you.' Too little, too late after all the pressure he'd applied.

Swallowing hard on the barbs she was dreaming up for Pike, she puts a hand on top of his, holding him in a gaze that makes him stiffen in his seat. Pike's mouth works, lost this once for words, then breaks into a grin.

They stay like that for five long seconds. She checks the door again and Rick is gone, jerks away her hand and rises without a word, leaving Brendan ten dollars by the till.

Out on the street, Pike comes waddling up behind, panting with what? Effort, lust?

She turns and says, 'Fuck off, Pike. Just. Fuck. Off.'

His face goes red and he starts to bluster.

She ducks into Silver Street and manages two-dozen steps before leaning against the wall. On the far side of the road, the homeless guy is coughing, yet to rise from his usual pile of cardboard. He looks comfortable, even carefree with his waist-length dreads rolled up, a felted pillow for his head. A psych colleague of Rick's had once said the guy's mind had gone as a result of bouncing off a train. It had been an endeavour he'd undertaken to relieve himself of childhood memories, of what he'd been forced to do in the Khmer Rouge camps.

Suzie looks at him and considers his success, comparing it to her own.

Wheelbarrow Ridge

She strolls along the footpath as he watches unseen, the sight of her jolting him out of time and place. Her fall of auburn hair, the particular glide in her step that belongs to someone else, someone long gone. How could it be? But when he recovers his bearings, he finds himself still out on the same old streets.

After the first sighting, he sees the new young woman around town with increasing frequency, observing a pram, a spouse: just as tall, nice coat. The driver wonders idly about their lives, if they are professionals moved up from the city. He savours his anonymity during these moments of observation. There's no harm in it, the shifts being long and customers scarce on the winter streets. It's better than thinking about his own life, choices made, unmade, leading here to the taxi rank. You know your streets, go unnoticed, it's better that way.

Moments of guilt gather as he feels the furtiveness of his discretion. Months pass and she never sees him watching. He concludes that he is in trouble, observing her from behind. From that angle, she could be the other one, the woman with one need left, to be forgotten.

He leads a solitary life. It feels like a confession when he talks about her to the other driver, Ken. Though he makes it sound casual. They wait for a fare at the rank, leaning on the warm bonnet of Ken's Ford. She walks up past the pub on the other side of the street, oblivious.

Nodding slightly in her direction, he says, 'Nice looking lass.'

Ken is not his friend. But as Ken's AA sponsor, there has to be some trust. And now he needs to talk. Ken's reply startles and disturbs the driver.

'Mate, she's not a bad looken piece, but she's gotta be trouble.'

The driver turns to face him, struggling for words that might sound casual.

Ken watches in turn, playing the older man's confusion like he holds it on a string. 'Mate,' he continues when he has had the upper hand long enough, 'that Goth she's with's gotta be a junkie.'

'Goth?' the driver replies, confused. In another life, he'd read a lot of history, until his own Decline and Fall.

'Mate, don't be stupid,' Ken continues. 'Sure he puts on the dog with his fancy coat, but it's still the uniform, you know, the all-in-black. And his bling, take a squiz sometime… Whadaya call that pentagram bullshit?'

The driver feels his weight of years as he considers Ken's pronouncement. Goth! He mulls the word, examining it within the context of this godforsaken town, seeing its fit. 'But,' he replies at last, 'what gives you the right to say the young fellow's a junkie?'

'Don't be stupid,' comes the reply. 'For a start, the guy's not young. Add his uniform to his age, multiply it by the ponytail and that makes him, you know, phase-locked. They're all the same, junkies. Ya wanna know when they got addicted, check out their dress sense.' Ken snorts, amused by the superiority of his insight.

The figure of the woman dwindles. Yes, she is younger than her spouse.

The driver looks up at the first stars, pulling his jacket tight against the settling chill. 'Yeah, right Ken, sure,' he says, walking back to his car. Ken is a jackass. That doesn't make him wrong.

He starts the engine to get the heater going. It runs rough and stalls. He hisses a string of curses, ending in a woman's name. Then, wrenching his mind's eye clear of auburn hair, sees instead her streaming cheeks, stained with run mascara. Beyond them is a bottle of gin. He restarts the engine, drives back to base and tells Rhonda that he's sick. It's many years since he gave up the drink, but it hasn't given up on him. And now, with this pressure of unwanted memory, he can feel the seal begin to crack. He has to get away, out to his shack in the empty spaces beyond the Wheelbarrow Ridge.

Two hotels and a bottle shop separate him from the safety of Wheelbarrow Ridge Road. Turning off at last, he leans back into his seat and sighs, driving slowly up past the lookout, watching for kangaroos on the edge of high beam.

After that day, the driver feels an aversion for Ken. He has odd chats with Rhonda in the mornings, ignores the customers and keeps tight within himself. If he sees the young woman, he turns away, looks at the last digit on the odometer and mentally sorts the stanzas of Tennyson's 'Ulysses', reciting the same-numbered verse.

Time passes, the flowering cherries on Main Street weigh heavy with spring blossom, he feels that he is better. Then, beyond a confetti swirl of fallen petals, below a velvet dusk on the edge of town, life falls hard on the driver. The house in his headlights is neat, a cheapo built to demountable standards. A silver copse of mountain ash crowds over it. Towering into the dark, they have dropped a raft of leaf and stick onto the low-angled roof.

He pulls into the driveway and the flat-lit door opens onto a sliver of domestic darkness. Suddenly, the door jerks shut then shudders from a violent impact within. It looks bad. He throws the taxi into reverse but sees the door re-open wide. She is there, peering into his lights with a hand raised, crying. The driver does not think, he gets out and walks in haste to the house, crunching gravel underfoot. There is a grinding in his heart like murder.

When he arrives at the steps, she is gone and he is looking up at the Goth, a sight so pathetic that his rage retreats into a colder, darker place. One arm is in plaster, the other hand in a clumsy bandage.

He holds both up, bawling, 'I just need a fucken ambulance and they've left me hangen. Get me to the fucken hospital. God, I need help.' He goes to punch the door again with his bandaged hand and the girl appears, mascara running down her cheeks, holding him back as she sobs.

Beyond the door the baby totters, reaching for its mother. The driver sees his past swung open. He fears he'll see himself lurch through; he knows what he'd do next.

He steps back. The Goth takes this as a cue, limping past him, opening the taxi door with a whimper, crawling in. The driver finds her standing over him, that same height, holding the toddler on her hip, just like the other.

'I'm sorry,' the young woman says. 'He was badly beaten and they've broken his arm… He's tried so hard but can't bear the pain…' She starts sobbing again.

The driver edges away. One day at a time, twenty hollow years, what good when they might collapse at any moment? There is a single thing to be done, take the Goth.

He pauses at the end of the street, wondering where to turn: the hospital…the sandy soils of Wheelbarrow Ridge. Rhonda crackles onto the air, peeved. She's had insistent calls from the pick-up in that street and wonders, what's his status, what has he been doing? The driver takes the mike and acknowledges, spinning his wheel towards the hospital.

The Goth begins a monologue, complaining that medical staff don't understand his pain, that they lack compassion.

The driver asks, 'You already been to the hospital?'

The Goth replies that now he's hurt his hand they'll have to help him.

'With morphine?' the driver adds, needing no reply.

The next morning, he calls in sick and paces round his shack. Rhonda makes remarks about a need for younger drivers, but today there is a gauntlet of liquor outlets he dares not run. Yet, in every dusty corner of the shack, accusations stir. The woman of his past stands silent, a shadow in the corner. He closes the door behind him and walks across the tussock flat on which the shack is built.

Yarns of web and diamond dew smear his sodden legs. Crossing to a forest floor, dry leaf crackles underfoot. His wheeze adopts a rhythm as he climbs towards the ridge. At valley's head there is a small escarpment, and in the back a cave.

A bundle of kindling and dry sticks sit atop a sandy ledge and he uses his cigarette lighter to get a fire going. Pulling down a dusty blanket he shakes it free of scats and sand, drapes it round his shoulders and sits to dry his legs. The sun has climbed above the tussock and he watches it steam the wet clumps. Ghosts of vapour whorl and disappear.

Rhonda gives him another chance and he plies the streets diligently. At the book exchange he finds a copy of *The Rhyme of the Ancient Mariner* and studies it hard at the rank, learning stanza after stanza. He hopes not to see the couple and, being successful, wonders if they've moved.

Yet memories seep between the stanzas and he wonders about his lover, whether the baby survived and where it might be now, one way or the other. Dragging his mind back to the book, he reads of thirst but thinks of drink: it would be so easy, the bottle a consolation, the beginning of an end. He despises himself and drives the drunkards home.

One day as he mutters verse, an alarmed matron demands he stop the taxi. Outside the pub he tries in vain to hand her change as she hobbles out of reach. At that moment, the Goth comes, cutting a smart figure past the hotel shopfront. Despite his carefree appearance, the driver sees him peer furtively through each window he passes. At the far end of the building, he spins around and creeps up to a door. Leaning cautiously through, he hesitates, then disappears inside.

The driver swings his vehicle into the taxi rank across the street and heads over to the pub. Inside, a chubby tracksuit walks away from the Goth, who is heading for the toilets. The driver follows and a cubicle door clicks shut as he enters. There is an empty wine bottle on the bench and he picks it up and leans flat against the tiled wall next to the cubicle, clutching the bottle by its neck. The tiles are cool against his back.

When the Goth reappears, he has lost all caution. Languidly, he steps towards the mirror. The driver comes in behind, raising the bottle as the Goth looks up at their reflection. The driver sees the image too, faces aligned in stupor and rage. He lowers the bottle and it clangs to the floor.

He lasts another week. A final intoxicated passenger floods his taxi with the stink of bourbon vomit. Scraping spew off the upholstery is a final straw. The shift done, he makes it past two hotels then swerves in to the bottle shop, buying the biggest bottle of gin they have.

Bottle on lap, he brims anticipation. Slewing gravel at the turn-off, he speeds between the switchbacks. At the ridge, treetops burnished by an evening sun, he glances to the lookout. There, a couple sit atop a picnic table, young lovers, oblivious to the world. A boy faces the road, good-looking, a stranger. The girl on his lap is holding his shoulders at arm's length, staring straight into his face. Her back is to the road but the driver knows her instantly. The boy's face radiates such happiness. The driver sobs.

He accelerates onwards, towards the creek, where apple gums have broken into blossom. With the window down, he catches the scent. On the straight before the bridge, he cracks the seal of the screw cap, flinging the bottle over the railing as he passes.

www.ingramcontent.com/pod-product-compliance
Lightning Source LLC
Chambersburg PA
CBHW030212130726
47898CB00012B/999